"Does that mean you've already decided what it is you want to do?"

He looked at her levelly, his gray eyes fixed on her. "I want a son," he stated. "I would prefer not to marry, but since I need to protect my parental rights, I'm prepared to make a temporary marriage. You have reasons, too, for wanting a marriage certificate. A brief marriage to each other would, I believe, suit us both."

Elexa swallowed. There it was. Noah Peverelle had just offered to marry her. She wasn't ready to say yes, she knew she wasn't. "You mentioned giving me time to think everything through...."

He was already getting to his feet, prepared to leave, when he asked, "If there's nothing further you want to know?"

"I wouldn't have to live with you?" she blurted out.

To her astonishment, he stated, "Beautiful though you undoubtedly are, Elexa, I'd prefer that you didn't."

To have and to hold...

Their marriage was meant to last—
and they have the gold rings to prove it!

To love and to cherish...

But what happens when their promise
to love, honor and cherish is put to the test?

From this day forward...

Emotions run high as husbands and wives discover
how precious—and fragile—their wedding vows are....
Will true love keep them together—forever?

Marriages meant to last!

PART-TIME MARRIAGE
Jessica Steele

TORONTO • NEW YORK • LONDON
AMSTERDAM • PARIS • SYDNEY • HAMBURG
STOCKHOLM • ATHENS • TOKYO • MILAN • MADRID
PRAGUE • WARSAW • BUDAPEST • AUCKLAND

ISBN 0-373-03680-9

PART-TIME MARRIAGE

First North American Publication 2001.

This edition published by arrangement with Harlequin Books S.A.

® and TM are trademarks of the publisher. Trademarks indicated with
® are registered in the United States Patent and Trademark Office, the
Canadian Trade Marks Office and in other countries.

Visit us at www.eHarlequin.com

Printed in U.S.A.

CHAPTER ONE

THERE were too many complications in her life! Elexa's mood to complete the work she'd brought home was sorely shattered as she stared at the phone after her mother's call and felt on the brink of doing something drastic.

Life should have been something of a breeze, and would be, were it not for her 'family' and, to a lesser degree, 'men', well-meaning in the main though they meant to be—only she wished that they wouldn't.

Why couldn't they see that she was happy and contented with her lot? She had an excellent job with Colman and Fisher, a name well known in the marketing world, and at twenty-five she was already a team leader in the market planning division, with every chance of going higher. So who needed a boyfriend, a lover, a husband?

Jamie Hodges was forever hoping to fill the position of her steady boyfriend. She was running out of excuses not to go out with him. With Des Reynolds she hadn't bothered making excuses when, in his sexiest voice, he'd suggested that one night with him and she'd never be the same again. 'In your dreams!' she'd told him bluntly—but that hadn't stopped him.

But although she found both men's persistence wearing, it was her mother's dogged insistence that at 'her age' she should by now be 'settled' that was the most wearing of all.

'I *am* settled!' she'd attempted to get through to her mother. 'I've got a good job, a job I love. A job with endless opportunities for promo—'

'I'm not talking that kind of settled,' her mother had interrupted.

Elexa knew exactly what kind of settled her mother meant. Married, nice house in the country, children—particularly children; even before her cousin Joanna had produced an offspring Elexa's mother had been desperate to become a grandmother. Since the arrival of baby Betsy, Kaye Aston had been ten times worse. Elexa had tried explaining matters to her, explaining how she already had her own home. So, okay, it was a flat and not a house, and it was in London and not in the country, but, given that she rented her flat, she had made it her own. She had tried explaining that she was enjoying her career too much to even want to think of marriage, much less settle down to that state.

The result of this heart-to-heart had been that, ignoring the possibility that any daughter of hers—even as academically bright as her daughter had shown herself to be—could be so totally dedicated to a career, her mother had grown terribly anxious and was now certain that Elexa must have suffered some extremely painful experience. An experience which she had kept quiet about, but which must have put her off men. Kaye Aston had refused to believe otherwise and had since taken to introducing Elexa to 'gentle' men—who invariably turned out to be 'drippy' men!

Elexa had moved from her old home and into her present flat a few years ago. But, apart from some family gathering or other—more frequent of late—she was expected to return and visit her parents on average every three weeks. Because she loved her parents, Elexa willingly complied, and had been happy to do so.

But that had been then, before her cousin Joanna had firstly become engaged and subsequently had married; that

Elexa's younger cousin had married first had not gone down well. Kaye Aston had not lost the opportunity to tell Elexa of her disappointment, and since Joanna and David had produced baby Betsy Elexa's mother seemed to have only one topic of conversation.

Elexa had started to dread her mother's phone calls. But she had begun to dread even more her once-every-three-weeks visits to her old home, never knowing what man it would be this time. Where her mother found them from was a mystery to Elexa—she must have her scouts out searching!

Kaye Aston's phone call just now had been to remind her, at length, that it was baby Betsy's christening this coming Sunday. 'You remember Thomas Fielding?' her mother had asked. 'Now isn't it kind?' she'd rushed on. 'Joanna has invited him to the party afterwards.'

Tommy Fielding was a man Elexa had known for years, a man who was about the same age as herself and was another 'gentle' soul. No need to ask why her mother had wangled an invitation for him. Worse, Elexa saw Aunt Celia's hand in this. Aunt Celia, one of her mother's two sisters, was Joanna's mother. Quite clearly Aunt Celia had been roped in to cajole Joanna into issuing the invitation. Which, in turn, Elexa suddenly realised, must mean that Joanna as well as Aunt Celia had joined in the 'Let's get Elexa married' campaign.

Feeling at her wits' end, Elexa knew all too well that to try again to explain that she had not endured any painful experience would be like banging her head against a brick wall. Countless were the times she had tried to get through that she found her work far more interesting than any man she had come across. She had lost count of the times she had explained that she just *did not want to be married*, and that she had no desire to leave her well-paid career to set up home with some gentle soul like Tommy Fielding who, nice, sweet as he was—as they all were—would want her to play 'wife', and would be unbearably hurt to discover that she had a career she preferred to staying home and playing house.

Suddenly, and as abruptly, Elexa all at once knew she had had enough. She was aware that her mother worried about her, but, feeling backed into a corner with no way out, Elexa just knew she could not take any more of it. She had tried, endlessly tried, explaining to her mother that she was not interested in 'settling down', and that her career had priority over everything. What had been the result? Even more pressure, and with back-up forces.

Well, she wasn't having it. Elexa pushed distraught fingers through her pale gold-lit blonde hair. But what could she do about it? All she craved was a year free of the relentless pressure—there was chance of promotion in the not-too-distant future. She just wanted time to concentrate all her spare energies on that.

She sighed and stared unseeing across the room, and then—perhaps born of utter desperation, but entirely unbidden—she was suddenly recalling again the conversation she had overheard about a month ago. It had been one lunchtime and she had been waiting for her friend Lois Crosby to join her. Lois was always late.

She and Lois were meeting to have lunch at the Montgomery, and, as busy as Elexa always was, she had been first there. The head waiter had led her to a series of sectioned-off booths, designed so that business people could lunch in the smart restaurant and be able to converse in relative privacy to discuss their business.

Elexa sometimes entertained clients at the Montgomery and, her name—or possibly her face—recognised, she had been left with a menu and the drink she had ordered to wait for her guest.

She'd had her back to the adjoining booth, but whatever she had been thinking about—either work, or Lois and, it was not unlikely, family pressures—had gone from her head when she had become aware that the previous lone occupant of the booth behind had company.

'Noah!' greeted one.

'Marcus,' answered the other.

She guessed they had shaken hands, and glanced to the large mirror facing her and saw reflected that a tallish fair-haired man had risen to greet a taller dark-haired man. They were both somewhere in their middle thirties, both immaculately suited, and businessmen. They exchanged a few comments with two distinct voices, one low and well modulated, the other lighter. Then they were sitting down out of her view—but not out of her hearing.

'We don't seem to have seen anything of you in the two years since you became international chairman.' That was the lighter voice—Marcus's voice, she thought.

'I hear you're doing well at Stanton's.' Noah? Noah obviously felt no need to boast about being international chairman, but was interested to hear how his lunch companion was getting on.

'Not without cost,' Marcus replied.

Silence—maybe they were studying menus. 'What cost would that be?' Noah asked idly.

'Family. I hardly ever see my children,' Marcus stated.

Elexa supposed she must have nipped out of their conversation to occupy herself with her own thoughts for a while, because when she had next become aware of their conversation she had been able to gather that they were obviously good friends who hadn't seen each other in an age and were still catching up, with Marcus accusing Noah of being the same old workaholic.

'Not without cost.' She heard Noah bounce back the same phrase Marcus had used earlier.

'How so?'

She guessed at that point that Noah must have given a shrug or something of the sort. There had been a pause anyway for a few moments, before, 'There's a price you pay for everything, Marcus,' he said. 'With me it's not having time to have a family.'

'You want a family?' Marcus sounded incredulous. 'You want a wife and—'

'I don't particularly want a wife,' Noah cut him off. 'In fact, to be frank, a wife is an appendage I can well do without.' A pause, then, 'Though I have been wondering just lately what it is I'm striving for.'

'You can't get much higher than international chairman.'

There was a second or two's silence, and she visualised Noah giving another shrug. Then he was saying, 'Don't get me wrong. I enjoy my work, the challenges it brings day to day. But...'

'But something's lacking?' Marcus put in.

There was a short silence, then Noah was saying something about having been taking stock, something about more to life than being successful in business, and admitting, 'A son. I've been thinking for a month or two now that I would quite like to have a son.'

'You, with children?' Marcus seemed surprised.

'One would be sufficient.'

'I thought you were a confirmed bachelor?'

'I am, but I'd be prepared to give up that status—briefly,' he qualified.

This time it was Marcus who paused. 'You never cease

to amaze me, Noah! At university you were always able to think on a different planet from the rest of us.' Elexa heard a smile in Marcus's voice. 'Now you want a part-time wife!'

'I don't want a wife at all!' Noah put him straight without delay. 'But to have a son I'd have to get temporarily tied to some woman.' Marcus made some kind of ribbing statement, then Noah was proclaiming, 'Find me a woman who's willing to marry, produce and then divorce, and I might think about it.'

'You're serious?' Marcus wanted to know. 'You think she exists—this woman who's going to produce your heir and then cheerfully disappear?'

'I've neither space for emotional entanglements nor time to go hunting,' Noah answered.

'You're still constantly on the move?'

Elexa guessed Noah had given some affirmative kind of nod, for he was then going on, 'According to my work schedule I land round about three years next Palm Sunday.' There was the sound of male laughter.

Then Marcus was suggesting, 'Why not sort a temporary wife out from your own stable?'

Like some brood mare! Elexa was not amused.

But apparently the up-to-his-eyes-in-work Noah knew quite a number of willing females. He admitted as much when he answered, 'You've met some of them. Can you honestly see any of them being content to present me with Peverelle junior and then, regardless of any financial settlement we agreed in advance, going quietly?'

'Whooh! Very shaky ground,' Marcus conceded, but at that point, glancing in the huge mirror in front, Elexa saw that her friend had arrived and was being directed her way.

Elexa might not have given the overheard conversation another moment's thought—after all she knew neither of the men. But her friend Lois had—at least she knew one of them. Tall and attractive, she obviously recognised one of the men in the adjoining booth, and paused in passing.

'*Bon appetit*, Marcus,' she greeted with the grin of an old friend.

Marcus was already on his feet. 'You still slaying them at that financial institution?' he enquired, kissing her cheek, referring to the finance house she worked for.

'Earning a crust,' she acknowledged, the outfit she was wearing suggesting it was a well-buttered crust.

'You don't know Noah Peverelle?'

The tall dark-haired man was on his feet too, and Elexa took more note of this man who wanted a son but didn't want a wife. She quickly dropped her gaze, however, when, having replied to his friend's introduction, Noah Peverelle seemed to become aware that someone was watching him. Fleetingly, before she looked down, her large brown eyes made contact with a pair of grey eyes.

Then Lois was joining her, apologising profusely for being late, explaining that she hadn't been able to get away from her client. 'Don't give it another thought,' Elexa excused her, but, aware how easily she had overheard the conversation in the next booth, for all neither man had been speaking loudly, she was careful to keep her chat with Lois light.

The two men were the first to leave. 'How's your mother?' Lois was asking. 'Still trying to get you married off?'

'You're about the only one I know who isn't trying,' Elexa replied, her thoughts on her aunt Celia and her cousin.

'Ah, but I've been there, done that—and wouldn't recommend it,' Lois answered, newly divorced and happy to be out of a bad marriage.

'Er—who's Marcus?' Elexa asked. She and Lois had been at school together and could ask each other anything—and Lois, either through her personality or her work, seemed to know practically everybody.

'Marcus—as in Marcus just now, having lunch with no less a personage than Noah Peverelle?'

'You know Noah Peverelle too?'

'Until today had never met him. But knew of his reputation,' Lois answered, speaking in the shorthand of old friends. 'He's the big noise over at the Samara Group— you know them; they're that international communications company, they've offshoots all over the place.'

Elexa had never got to hear more about Marcus, because a cursory glance at her watch had made her exclaim in a hurry, 'I've got to dash! I've a meeting I'm going to be late for if I don't get my skates on.'

She had seen Lois since. They had shopped together a couple of weeks ago, and had lunch together only last week. But neither the name of Marcus, whoever he was, or Noah Peverelle had come up again. Though Elexa had thought of that overheard conversation quite a number of times.

She had equally dismissed the overheard conversation too as being the sort of thing you said to a friend you knew well without being expected to be taken seriously.

But now, after her mother's latest phone call, pushed into a seemingly no-way-out kind of corner, and with the prospect hanging over her of Tommy Fielding—and after him, without a doubt, someone else, and so on *ad infinitum*—Elexa just had to wonder, *had* Noah Peverelle been serious? On thinking about it, she felt that he had *sounded* serious, deadly serious. But...

It was absurd! She'd never have the nerve—her stomach started to churn at the very idea. Elexa attempted to dismiss the notion. But the pressure was on, that pressure strengthening, and, short of caving in and taking on one of her mother's 'nice' types, what was a career minded executive to do?

She had tried the heart-to-heart with her mother—it had only made matters worse. She knew that her mother worried about her—she was a natural born worrier. In fact Elexa's father had often said that if her mother didn't have anything to worry about she would invent something. But this roping in Joanna, along with Aunt Celia, was going *too* far.

Yes, but to contemplate marrying some stranger, having his baby and then divorcing just to get her well-meaning relatives off her back, was a bit desperate, wasn't it?

But the situation *was* desperate! On impulse Elexa picked up the phone and dialled her friend Lois's number. It was ridiculous, Elexa decided, before the number had started ringing out.

So why didn't she put down the phone? Gentle, nice Tommy Fielding and a string of others like him, that was why, Elexa answered her own question. *And* there was that prospect of promotion she should be concentrating on—instead of evading her mother's water-wearing-away-stone tactics.

'Elexa!' Lois exclaimed when she heard her voice. 'I was just thinking about you and wondering if you fancy doing anything at the weekend.'

'It's the christening this weekend,' Elexa reminded her friend. Lois had often stayed weekends in Elexa's home when they had been schoolgirls, and knew all of Elexa's family.

'Joanna's sprog?'

'She's rather cute,' Elexa replied—and brought herself up short. Good heavens, where had that come from? She wasn't getting all mumsie, was she? Just because she had been toying with some far-fetched idea of having a baby, she wasn't going all broody, was she? 'Er—I need a favour,' she said quickly.

'If it's in my power, it's yours,' Lois answered without hesitation.

'You don't know what it is yet,' Elexa laughed. But even as she laughed, she knew that she was delaying asking the question because she didn't want to ask it. It was as if, once asked, it would commit her to carrying through her only half-thought-out plan.

'If I know you, it won't be anything too diabolical. Give?' Lois requested.

'I—er...' Lois was her oldest and most trusted friend, Elexa reminded herself. 'I—um—need Noah Peverelle's private number,' she plunged. 'And I can't tell you why,' she added hastily.

There followed a small silence. 'Intriguing,' Lois ruminated. 'But,' she added after a moment, 'I don't know it. I only ever met him that one time. Uh!' she exclaimed. 'You know that I know a man who may know it, right?'

'Marcus and Noah Peverelle are great friends,' Elexa volunteered.

'You sound as if you know them both very well,' Lois opined.

'I don't,' Elexa had to confess. 'Is there a chance you could ask Marcus without telling him why you need Noah's number?'

'If they're such good friends, Marcus Dean isn't going to tell me without wanting to know why,' Lois commented. 'Hang on, though. Ginny Dean owes me a favour! I'll ring Marcus's wife and get back to you.'

Elexa put down her phone after her call, wondering what she had done. She had involved Lois in something which

Elexa wasn't certain she was going to take any further anyway.

Though, in thinking about it more deeply, more logically, instead of panicking that family pressures had become too intense past bearing, she suddenly realised that, while her career was all-important, yes, there was every probability that she would at some stage rather like to have a child.

It shook Elexa a little that she had child-bearing instincts. It was something she had never considered before. But, in delving more deeply, she recalled how, when Joanna had given her the baby to hold one time, she had been more than happy to nurse the sweet, sleeping infant in her arms.

For a few minutes Elexa lived with the discovery that she was no different from most other women—and that she did have the same maternal instincts. Then she gave herself a mental shaking—that still didn't mean that she wanted a husband. She most definitely did not. In her view they were vastly overrated.

Noah Peverelle wouldn't be your normal run-of-the-mill husband, though. For a start it sounded, with his talk of according to his work schedule he'd land round about three years next Palm Sunday, as if he wouldn't be around much anyway. Not that she had any intention of living with the man. And in any case, in three years' time she would be married and divorced from him. Not that she wanted to marry the man in the first place, but...

Elexa abruptly cut off her thoughts mid-stream. Good grief, woman, don't start making plans. You haven't so much as got his phone number yet, much less plucked up the courage it will take to suggest what you have to suggest. But—she was still feeling quite desperate, and desperate problems called for desperate solutions.

But what if Noah Peverelle hadn't been serious anyway? What kind of a fool would that make her look? What...? Elexa was just building up a fine head of steam against Noah Peverelle for daring to make her feel a fool when the phone rang.

She grabbed at it. But it wasn't Lois; it was her mother. It couldn't have been an hour ago that they had last spoken! It must be important. It was—to her mother. 'I forgot to ask. What are you going to wear on Sunday?'

'Wear?' Elexa repeated in surprise. 'Does it matter?'

'Of course it matters. You'll want to look your best when Tommy Fielding sees you again. I don't want you turning up in those old trousers you were wearing when Timothy Stowe popped round the other Sunday.'

Popped round! As Elexa recalled it—and she had been wearing a pair of fairly new trousers at the time—Timothy Stowe had been especially invited to 'pop' in to see her father's stamp collection, and to stay to tea. But Elexa knew from past experience that it would do no good to remind her mother of this. Timothy, Tommy—she'd probably got a Tarquin all lined up ready, should Tommy Fielding fail to thaw her annoying daughter's stony heart.

'I'll make sure to wear something smart,' Elexa replied finally, feeling too worn down by the constant attempts at coercion to want an argument with her parent.

'Good,' her mother replied, and rang off—no doubt, Elexa assumed, to do more scheming in the I'll-get-my-daughter-to-the-church-if-it's-the-last-thing-I-do stakes.

A minute later, however, and the phone rang again, and this time it was Lois. 'I've perjured my soul to get this for you,' Lois began. 'Have you got a pen handy?'

Elexa took down the number her good friend read out to her, and repeated it back, and then said gratefully, 'I truly appreciate it, Lois.'

'What are friends for? Though you'll have to tell me why you want it as soon as you can. My imagination is running riot, trying to guess what's going on!'

Elexa said goodbye to her, knowing that not even in her wildest imaginings would Lois ever guess at the truth of what was going on. That was, Elexa mused, beginning to feel hot all over at the thought of what she was contemplating, if she ever found enough nerve to call that number.

She did call it though, a half-hour later when she was heartily fed up with her dithering. For goodness' sake, the man hadn't space for emotional entanglements—well, neither had she! With her throat dry, her hands shaking, she picked up the phone and pressed out Noah Peverelle's number, and consequently didn't know whether she felt frustrated or relieved when he wasn't home.

He really was as busy as he'd intimated, she had to conclude when over the next couple of days she tried his number again with the same result. He was never home.

By Sunday morning it had become something of a fixture in her mind that she would keep ringing his number until he *did* answer. By then she knew his number off by heart and, just before she left her flat to drive to her parents' home in Berkshire, she stabbed out the digits again.

'Peverelle,' said a voice she knew—and Elexa only just managed to hold down a squeak of alarm.

It was *him*! *He!* 'Hello!' she managed, the whole idea of what she was about all at once seeming not only crazy but totally preposterous. Yet, as she recalled that her mother had again phoned her last night to ask her to be 'warm' to Tommy Fielding, Elexa saw that if she could manage to spit the rest of her rehearsed speech out, she might see in front of her time free of pressure—leaving her the space she craved to be left in peace to get on with her career. 'You don't know me—' She pushed herself to go on, but just couldn't get any further. It *was* preposterous! It was...

'Do you have a name?' Noah Peverelle asked shortly. Elexa made a face—charm school had obviously been wasted on him. But for the moment she preferred to stay anonymous.

'The thing is,' she asserted herself to begin briskly, 'that you would like a s-son, and I need a h-husband tem...' Temporarily, she would have said, had he given her the chance.

'Who the hell are you?' Peverelle demanded curtly.

'No one you know. We—'

'Where did you get hold of that sort of erroneous information?' he challenged sharply. 'Are you press?'

'No, I'm not!' she erupted, unsure if she was glad or sorry that her information was erroneous. Though, hang on—it wasn't erroneous. She had heard it herself from him with her very own ears. Abruptly then she realised that if he believed her to be from the newspapers he would automatically deny he had said any such thing, wouldn't he? 'We have a mutual friend, sort of,' she hurried on.

'Who?' he rapped.

Don't beat about the bush, come straight to the point, why don't you? 'That's not important just now.'

'So—what is important?'

'You sounded much more pleasant the last time I heard you talking,' Elexa said without thinking.

'I've had a hard week!' he rapped again, clearly taking in his stride that she, somewhere before, and at some time, had heard his voice. 'What are you after?'

'Nothing—other than...'

'A husband, in return for a son—and a meal ticket for the rest of your life, no doubt,' he snarled.

He thought she was after his wealth! Shocked, Elexa

was speechless for endless seconds. Then, furious with
him, with herself, 'When I'm that hard-up I'll let you
know!' she hissed, and fairly threw the phone back on its
rest. That anyone could accuse her of such a thing as marrying for money was something she had simply not considered.

To think she had seriously, for even half a moment,
thought of tying herself up with that suspicious swine! She
had money of her own without wanting any of his, thank
you very much. Her parents were quite well off, as too
had been her grandparents. They had left her a substantial
sum of money, sufficient anyway for her to be able to live
comfortably without the need to touch her not inconsid-
erable salary. Had *he* been mixing with the wrong sort of
woman? Suspicious devil!

Elexa was still fuming a minute later when her phone
rang for attention. She gave a hefty sigh of despair. She
would be seeing her mother quite soon now; she did not
really need another call from her with yet more instructions
on how she should behave with Tommy Fielding.

But, unable to give in to her mother and 'marry and
settle down', Elexa tried in other ways to be dutiful and
respectful, and went to answer the phone, hoping that her
parent would make it brief.

'Hello,' she said, and was shaken rigid to hear the voice
of the man upon whom she had just slammed the receiver
down.

'So what's with the proposition?' he said toughly.

Proposition! He thought, Mr Clever, dial one-four-
seven-one to get his last caller's number—so much for
wanting to remain anonymous—that she was propositioning him! 'Forget it!' she snapped furiously. 'I'd sooner
marry a man-eating shark!' With that she slammed the

phone down on him for a second time. If it rang again, mother or no mother, she just wasn't answering it.

The christening went off beautifully, with baby Betsy being little short of angelic. Aunts and uncles, nephews and nieces were all assembled, all female members queuing up to cuddle the tiny bundle.

She really was a sweetheart, Elexa mused, feeling all sort of squashy inside when her turn came to hold and croon to the gorgeous cherub. Glancing up, though, she saw her mother watching her, and hated that she was made to feel guilty for denying her grandparental status.

Joanna came up to her. 'She'll want changing, I expect. Shall I have her?' the proud mum asked, and as she came closer to take the baby from Elexa she said, 'Sorry about Tommy. I couldn't say no without offending your mother,' she apologised for inviting the man who, while for a brief moment absent, had otherwise been sticking like glue to Elexa's side ever since he'd arrived.

'Don't worry about it. He's—er—nice.'

'Nice,' Joanna mouthed silently, and they exchanged cousinly grins. But as Elexa gave the baby up to her, Joanna warned, 'I saw Aunt Kaye nailing Rory a little while ago—I shouldn't be at all surprised to see Tommy Fielding at cousin Rory's wedding in a couple of months' time.'

'Oh, grief,' Elexa groaned.

'Shall I get you some christening cake?' Tommy hovered the moment Joanna had gone.

'I've had some, Tommy, thanks,' Elexa answered, fast running out of innocent topics of conversation—she had a feeling Tommy would be asking her for a date before the afternoon was over—it would be less embarrassing for them both if she could head him off.

She thought she had been successful when, as the party

started to break up, and at her mother's instigation, she went down the front garden path with Tommy to his car. But only to find that she hadn't been as successful as she'd believed.

'Come out with me tonight?' Tommy blurted out the moment they were alone, every bit as though he had bottled it up all afternoon and somebody had just let the cork out.

'I—er...' Elexa tried hard for some gentle way to say no, and then to her own incredulity—and his, 'I can't, Tommy. I'm dating someone,' she heard herself say. And, fearing Tommy would press her further, she found she was adding, 'Long term.' And to her further amazement, and quite without her bidding, a picture came into her head of tall, dark-haired Noah Peverelle, standing the way he had been at the Montgomery that day.

'But—your mother...' Tommy was arguing, astounded.

Elexa gave herself a mental shake and banished that sharp, snarling brute—he had actually accused her of propositioning him!—out of her head.

'Um—my mother doesn't know.' She smiled at Tommy.

Only the very next morning she learned that Tommy Fielding wasn't as nice as everyone thought him. He'd sneaked on her. She found that out when at six o'clock her mother phoned her.

Thinking it must surely be an emergency for anyone to get her out of bed this early, Elexa dashed to the phone when it rang, only to hear her mother's voice, full of sweetness and pleasantness exclaiming, 'I know how you don't like phone calls at work, so I thought I'd get you before you started your day.'

Her mother was quite plainly in fine form. 'Is Dad all right?' Elexa asked swiftly.

'He's still in bed—old lazy bones. Now, what's this I

hear about you going steady with someone? I rang Tommy Fielding late last night, and he—'

'*Mother!*' At six o'clock in the morning! Was there to be no rest from it?

'I didn't ring you last night because Tommy said you were seeing your steady boyfriend.' Elexa was astonished her mother had waited this long! 'Now, tell me, what's his name and where you met him? And why on earth didn't you tell me?'

There wasn't a name, she hadn't met him, and there was nothing to tell—and Elexa felt very much like murdering Tommy Fielding. 'It's—er—all rather new.' She was lying, to her mother! Elexa could barely take in that she had been worn down to such an extent. 'Mother,' she began, 'I didn't tell you because...' There's nothing to tell, she would have said, given half a chance.

But her mother was butting in angrily before she could finish. 'You're not living with him, I hope?' she questioned frostily.

'Would I dare?'

'Don't take that tone with me, young lady!' Kaye Aston, regardless of her daughter's executive, self-supporting position, ordered sharply. 'Your father and I have brought you up with strict moral values. I'm not having any daughter of mine...'

'Don't worry, I'm not living with him,' Elexa mollified her outraged parent, and just couldn't believe that as the phone call ended, with her mother saying that she wanted to meet 'him' sooner rather than later, she had let her go without confessing that she had lied to Tommy and that there was no long-term boyfriend.

Elexa was glad that her job called for a high degree of concentration. But thoughts of the yet more pressure she would have earned herself from her mother tried to constantly get through. She would have to confess her lie, reluctant though she was to do so—she had a fairly certain idea that her mother would be on the phone the instant she arrived back at her flat that night, wanting a long cosy chat about 'him'.

A picture of Noah Peverelle shot into her head. Oh, clear off! She must have been mad to have telephoned him—but he hadn't sounded so unpleasant when she had overheard him in the Montgomery. True, he had been with a trusted friend. Goodbye, bad idea.

Elexa got on with her day, getting the best out of her team and spending time communicating with clients, solving problems as and when they arose. She was late leaving her office, and drove home wondering how, when she was said to have excellent judgement in the market planning division and to be little short of fantastic when it came to planning, it seemed she didn't appear to have one solitary skill when it came to solving her own problems.

She let herself into her apartment and went over to the phone and punched one-four-seven-one; her mother had phoned ten minutes ago.

Elexa made herself a cup of coffee, anticipating that at any moment now she would be summoned to the phone.

It was not the phone that rang for her attention, however, but, while she was mid-rehearsal with the best way to confess that there was no 'steady' man-friend, the outer door buzzer sounded.

She wasn't expecting anyone to call, but went to the intercom in the hall. 'Who is it?' she asked lightly, and nearly dropped dead with shock.

'Noah Peverelle,' answered a cool, not-at-all-friendly-sounding voice.

No! Brain-stunned, Elexa couldn't think for several seconds. Then, reeling from so unexpectedly hearing what she had just heard, and with thoughts of how in creation he had managed to find her—let alone *why* had he bothered to find her—Elexa made a tremendous effort to get herself together.

He was waiting for her to let him in. He had said his name, dropped his bombshell, and had nothing more he wanted to say apparently—until they were standing face to face.

She swallowed hard on a suddenly desert dry throat. 'You'd—better come up,' she invited—she had no option—and pressed the button to unlatch the downstairs front door, and wished more than she had wished anything in her life that she had never made that phone call to him yesterday.

But phoned him she had, and it was too late now for wishing—Noah Peverelle was on his way up to see her, and must have gone to quite some trouble to find her!

CHAPTER TWO

ELEXA was still gasping, still striving to hold down panic, when the man she had two minutes before decided she did not want to see after all rang the doorbell to her flat, announcing that he was right outside.

She gulped for air, her usual smart intelligence deserting her as she sought for some 'I'm sorry I bothered you, I shouldn't have, goodbye' kind of comment. She was certain he would ring her doorbell again if she did not soon dash to open the door. But he did not. He was controlled, this man, this stranger—heaven help us, had she really, truly, suggested to him that they made a baby together?

Elexa felt scarlet all over when, knowing that she couldn't stand there dithering all night, she went to the door, her sophisticated image fast starting to slip. Dressed in a smart two-piece—calf-length skirt and boxy top of sage-green—and with her long blonde gold-lit hair brushing her shoulders, she pulled back the door. But any phrase she might have been able to utter was lost when, before he stepped over her threshold, 'Alexandra Aston?' he enquired.

'My friends call me Elexa,' she answered, and felt stupid because she had. This man, this stern looking man, this steely, grey-eyed man was not her friend and was never likely to be. 'Er—you'd better come in,' she invited.

She led the way into her sitting-room. She didn't remember him being so stern looking. True, he hadn't actually been smiling when she'd seen his reflection in that mirror, but neither had he been scowling.

'Can I get you something?' Politeness of years pushed her on. 'A drink, a...?' Abruptly, she halted. 'How did you find me?' she changed tack to ask sharply.

'It wasn't difficult.'

He was tall. She was five feet nine herself and didn't like having to look up to him. 'Would you like to take a seat?'

He moved over to her sofa but did not sit down until she had taken the chair opposite. She saw his glance flick round her elegantly furnished room, and cancelled any top marks she might have given him for manners because of it. No doubt he was totting up her furnishings—along with the rental of her flat in the not unsmart apartment block—and assessing how much she would need for the upkeep of both.

'Without my job—which pays very well—I have private means,' she told him irately.

'Falling before you're pushed?' he queried—and she hated him, hated that she felt her lips twitch. She had rather jumped in there with both feet, hadn't she? She didn't smile, of course. Why should she? He was looking as grim-faced as ever. 'I'm aware of your financial circumstances,' he informed her coolly.

'You've had me investigated?' Elexa went shooting away from holding down a laugh to being outraged. 'How dare—?'

'You proposed yourself to be the mother of my child—did you think I wouldn't have you investigated?' He was actually *considering* the proposition? Her brown eyes widened as she stared thunderstruck at him. 'Are you always this cantankerous?' he enquired mildly, his all-seeing grey eyes steady on her.

Elexa took a deep breath. She was feeling less panicky than she had, but was still feeling very shaken. 'I'm nervous.' She opted for honesty. 'Your call, you coming here tonight, was, well, unexpected to say the least.'

'You mean you wouldn't have slammed the phone down on me a third time had I telephoned first?'

'You had no intention of phoning first—you wanted to catch me unaware, with my defences down,' she accused.

He neither agreed nor denied it, but instead, his serious grey eyes fixed on her eyes, he questioned toughly, 'Why is it so important for you to be married?'

She wanted to deny it was important at all, then roused herself—she wasn't having him coming here to her home and acting like some man in charge. 'Why is it so important to you to have a son?' she tossed back shortly.

'Did you miss that part?'

She coloured—he knew it all, didn't he? 'So I was eavesdropping. Not that I intended to—' She broke off. 'How did you find out—that I'd been listening to your conversation—that day? That it was me?'

He shrugged. 'Marcus Dean was the only person who knew of my thoughts on having a son.'

'Mmm,' Elexa murmured. 'You remembered where you were when you were discussing it with him?'

'Marcus wouldn't discuss it with anyone else,' Noah Peverelle asserted, with the same confidence that Elexa had that anything she discussed with her friend Lois would go no further. 'Since the voice that called me yesterday wasn't the voice of Lois Crosby...'

'You remembered Lois's voice?'

'I knew yesterday's voice wasn't hers. Which meant it had to be her brown-eyed companion.'

'You remembered my eyes?' she asked incredulously. 'But it was ages ago—we didn't even speak!'

'You obviously didn't forget me,' he lobbed back at her. 'Or, more precisely, my side of the conversation. So tell me why, since it doesn't appear you're in any urgent need of money, are you so keen to have a husband?'

'I'm not!' Elexa answered bluntly, but not yet ready to go into more detail. 'So you knew who it was who phoned you, but—' She broke off again. 'How *did* you find out— who I am, was, I mean? Your friend Marcus wouldn't know me. Ah! You rang Marcus and he rang Lois…' Her voice trailed off. 'That can't be right. Lois would have rung me to say…'

'I didn't have to call Marcus. My company does a lot of business with the Montgomery…'

He had no need to continue. 'You contacted the restaurant and asked who had reserved the booth next to yours that lunchtime.' Clever swine.

'None of this is at all important. You've just said you're no longer in urgent need of a husband.' He looked to be about to leave.

Elexa suddenly realised she had very mixed feelings about that. It seemed a very good idea that he should go and that she should forget that she had started this whole sorry business, but… 'I never wanted a husband at all,' she informed him. 'But I'm being pushed—' The phone starting to ring cut through what she was saying. She knew it would be her mother—and started to panic again. 'Can you hang on while I take this call?' she asked quickly, and didn't wait to see whether he would or not. Presenting him with her back, she went over to the telephone and picked it up.

'I was hoping you'd be home from work by now,' her mother's voice came briskly down the wires. 'Now, what's so dreadful about your man-friend that you couldn't tell me about him before?'

'There's nothing dreadful about him,' Elexa found herself answering, barely able to believe she was still carrying out this myth that there was someone she was going 'steady' with.

'Then why didn't you bring him to the christening yesterday?'

'He's—uh—busy,' Elexa replied. What am I doing? 'He's a very busy man.'

'He's not married! Tell me he's not married! You wouldn't go out with a married man. Don't tell me I've reared a daughter who would—'

'Mother!' Elexa cut off her tirade. 'I didn't bring him because he—um—puts a lot of hours in with his work.'

'What's his name? He does have a name?'

Oh, grief. Elexa hadn't heard any doors closing. If Noah Peverelle was still in earshot—and she couldn't blame him if he was; she had after all listened in to his conversation—then he would just love it if she gave her mother his name. 'Can I give you a ring later?' she asked, and, rushing on before her mother should ask why, 'He's—er—here now—um…'

'He's there with you now? Why didn't you say?'

'I—er…'

'Ring me before you go to bed tonight,' her mother instructed firmly. 'And you'd better bring him to dinner on Saturday.'

Elexa came away from the phone with her head spinning. She turned and saw that Noah Peverelle was still there. 'Oh, grief,' she sighed, and collapsed into the nearest chair.

But she was not to be allowed time to get herself back together, it seemed, for straight away Noah Peverelle was bombarding her. 'Why would you tell your mother anything about me? And don't deny it was me you were talking about.'

Elexa had just about had enough of him. 'It didn't have

to be you; any man would have done,' she snapped, but wearily felt obliged to explain. 'Yesterday, in order to put somebody off, I invented having a steady boyfriend. He told my mother—she now wants me to bring said steady boyfriend to dinner on Saturday.'

'You look as fed up as you sound,' Noah Peverelle observed, and added speculatively, but nonetheless accurately, 'It's your mother who wants you to be married, not you, isn't it?'

Elexa didn't want to be disloyal to her mother, but somehow, having been driven to this situation by her, she was feeling just a little too worn down just then to mind so much.

'I don't need marriage. I've got a super job, excellent prospects of promotion—I'm more than happy with my career.'

'But your mother isn't?'

Elexa sighed. 'I've tried to explain how it is.'

'You can't have tried very hard.'

She felt like hitting him. 'Much you know! I tried so hard my mother is now convinced that some man has caused me so much pain that I'm off men for good—and that I'm never likely to marry. Now various old friends, and new acquaintances, are invited to my parents' home when I'm due to make a visit, and to family get-togethers—and I'm instructed to be nice to them.'

'Yesterday's offering being the one whom you told you were going steady?'

Elexa looked across at the unsmiling—rather good look-ing, she realised—dark-haired man occupying her sofa, re-cognising just how astute he was. It hadn't taken him any time at all to sort through the situation.

'It seemed the better way of saving his face when he asked me to go out with him.' Noah Peverelle gave her a look as if to say the sophisticated image she was trying for had slipped a mile and he had just glimpsed her softer centre. 'For my sins,' she went on, not liking that he had observed her softer side, 'he told my mother I was going steady.'

'She must have been pleased.'

Sarcastic devil! Again, though, Elexa felt an urge to laugh. Most odd. All this stress must be making her light-headed. 'My mother phoned me at six this morning wanting to know more about it.'

'It's getting you down?'

'You could say that.'

'Why not marry one of these men and be done with it?' Peverelle demanded.

Nothing like being told he'd rather drink burning oil than marry her himself, Elexa thought sniffily. And went on to think, Well, who asked you? But she more or less had. 'Because they would want to be emotionally involved.'

'And you don't?'

'All I want is time free of my mother being on the phone every five minutes. All I want is to be left alone to get on with the career I love. Don't get me wrong, I love my family, love my mother dearly, and I'd do anything for her but...'

'But marry some man on a permanent basis?'

'That's about it,' she had to agree, and looked steadily at the grey-eyed man across from her.

As she stared at Noah Peverelle, so he scrutinised her. She would have dearly liked to have known what was going through his mind, but guessed he would only let her know what he wanted her to know.

But, when she was thinking that he was probably considering he had wasted enough time and was about to leave, he surprised her by asking, 'How do you feel about children?'

Oh, help, was he really, *seriously* considering...? Had she *seriously* proposed what she had to this cold, unsmiling man? She wanted to swallow, but wouldn't, but, since he seemed such a forthright person, she gave his question serious thought, and answered honestly, 'Up until the day I heard you talking about having a son, I hadn't given children a thought—having them, that is. The furtherance of my career is important to me, as I mentioned. But, on thinking about children, I've realised that, while marriage has never featured in my plans, ultimately I shouldn't like to miss out and never have a child.'

She didn't know what she expected him to say to that. But discovered that he was clearly a most decisive man when, getting to his feet he informed her, 'I'm away from home for the rest of this week. Presumably your mother isn't too far away. What time shall I pick you up on Saturday?'

Elexa wasn't sure her jaw didn't drop. 'You're—you're coming to dinner with me at my parents' on Saturday?' she questioned, only just holding down a gasp of shock. Decisive, had she said?

'I'm not yet ready to be engaged to you—we need to discuss this more thoroughly first, and I'm already running late for another appointment. But I don't mind being your "steady" in the meantime.'

'Don't do me any favours!' she snapped huffily.

Noah Peverelle looked arrogantly down at her. 'We're in the territory of mutual favours here!' he rapped.

'So call for me at six-thirty!' she flared, and felt as if she'd just been poleaxed when, with nothing more than a curt nod, Noah Peverelle strode from her apartment.

How long she sat there, stunned that Noah Peverelle had

actually been inside her flat, had asked her a few short and to the point questions, and had then gone on to keep an appointment, Elexa had no idea.

But slowly, as she got herself into more of one piece, it began to dawn on her that with Peverelle's talk of mutual favours it rather looked—future discussions going well— as if they could be on the way to him marrying her, and to her giving him the son he wanted.

Oh, heck. Ice encased her southernmost extremities but, knowing that her mother was probably sitting by the phone, waiting for her to ring, this was no time to start getting cold feet. He, Peverelle, when all was said and done, had not been the one to approach her with the idea. Rather it had been she who had made the first approach.

Nevertheless, there were several occasions before Saturday arrived when Elexa came within an ace of contacting Noah Peverelle and telling him to forget the whole idea. Two things were against that, however. One was that he was away from home for the rest of the week—she didn't think he'd appreciate her phoning his office and leaving any kind of 'Would-you-tell-Mr-Peverelle-I've-decided-not-to-have-his-baby?' type of message. The very big other was that her mother was so excited about actually meeting her steady boyfriend she was never off the phone.

Worse, having been more or less forced to give her his name, her father too had been on the phone. Was her steady boyfriend *the* Noah Peverelle? Apparently her businessman father, who daily kept up to date with business news, knew all about what went on in *big* business, seemed as eager as her mother to meet him.

As, too, did Aunt Celia and Uncle Kenneth want to meet him. Aunt Celia had rung saying how delighted she was to hear her news. 'We're not engaged, or anything like that!' Elexa had told her hurriedly.

'No, but I know you, you wouldn't be taking him home to meet your parents unless you were serious about him.'

As far as Elexa could remember, she hadn't had any choice. Her mother had decreed 'dinner' and, while Elexa might have wriggled out of it, the lofty Peverelle—no doubt wanting to see what sort of stock she came from— had agreed, without being asked, to go to her parents' home with her.

At that point she came close to contacting his office and leaving a message to the effect that Saturday's arrangements had been cancelled. She objected strongly to him giving her parents the once-over. Though since, on reflection that was what her parents were doing, giving *him* the once-over to see if *he* was suitable for their only child, Elexa realised she hadn't got very much to complain about.

The only relief Elexa found from the tangle her private life seemed to be in was at her office. But even there she wasn't left in peace to do the job she so loved.

'I didn't see you at all yesterday,' Jamie Hodges interrupted her day to complain.

'I had several meetings—was it something specific?' she enquired, feeling pretty certain that she knew what was coming.

'I've got two tickets for the theatre on Saturday. I wondered if you were free?' he began eagerly.

'I'm not,' she replied, and knew she was as soft as Peverelle no doubt thought her because she couldn't tell Jamie more bluntly that he was wasting his time. She did not have the same problem in telling Des Reynolds to leave her alone, however.

'How's the most gorgeous woman ever to grace the portals of Colman and Fisher?' he leered, perching himself on a corner of her desk.

'Save it for your wife, Des. I'm up to my ears in—'

'Very beautiful ears, if I may...'

'I swear somebody turns a key and winds you up every morning.' She had to laugh. 'Clear off, Des, there's a good lad.' He went, and she supposed he would probably not change very much even if she did tell him she had a steady boyfriend. Jamie Hodges, now *he* was a different matter.

Elexa was halfway through rehearsing how she would tell Jamie that she was going out with someone she was going to marry when she stopped dead, her stomach churning. Apart from the fact he was a long way from agreeing yet, how could she contemplate marrying Peverelle? She didn't even like him! The thought of actually going to bed with the cold unfeeling brute was impossible.

Again Elexa was ready to pick up the phone and leave a message with his office. Her hand actually went to the phone—she pulled it back. Hang on just a minute! Wasn't that exactly what she wanted—a no-commitment kind of commitment?

By the time she returned to her flat that evening Elexa had been through again and again everything she wanted, and what she was going to have to do to get it. She had heard today the manager's job that had been rumoured, was definitely going to be announced shortly. It wasn't a senior manager's job—that would be some years away— but it was a job she wanted. Without false modesty, Elexa felt she was good enough to get it. She worked now in a high stress area—and loved it. But she knew there would be more pressure attached to the new job; she wouldn't need any extra in the shape of her family trying to push her into marriage.

So, the answer seemed obvious. Go through a marriage ceremony with Peverelle, get 'the other business' over and done with, and get back to what she was good at.

Her phone rang; she jumped. Her mother? Or—him?

Why him? Probably because she had thought so frequently of making a phone call to Peverelle. Was he making that phone call to her? How *dared* he? Feeling slightly miffed—that phone call was her prerogative—she picked up the phone and said a firm, 'Hello,' and discovered it wasn't him at all, but was her mother's other sister.

'I've only just heard about you and your man-friend,' her aunt Helen trilled. 'Now, you'll be sure to bring him to Rory's wedding, won't you? If you'll give me his address I'll be sure he gets an invitation.'

'I—er...' Oh, Lord. 'We'll look forward to it—um—thank you very much, Aunty,' Elexa replied—what else could she have said? 'Er—don't bother with a written invite.' She hadn't a clue about Peverelle's address.

'You'll be sure to tell him how welcome he is—how we're all dying to meet him?'

'I'll tell him,' Elexa assured her, and came off the phone sighing. Heavens above, the way the family were carrying on you'd think that she had never had a boyfriend and that Peverelle was her last chance!

By Saturday morning Elexa had convinced herself that she was taking a right and proper course of action. It was an unusual arrangement, of course. She accepted that. But when all this initial trauma was done and dusted and—subject to her and Peverelle agreeing on everything—then he would have the promise of an heir, and she would have the promise of some space to concentrate on what she so enjoyed: a career without constant family pressure. A year, that was all she craved. To think, in a year's time, she could have that all-important junior manager's job! And from there—who knew? The possibilities were limitless.

By six o'clock that evening, however, Elexa was having to firmly remind herself of all the reasons for why she was taking this course of action. When the outer door buzzer sounded a half an hour later she was feeling so all over the place that she could barely remember one good reason.

She saw no point in going to the intercom to ask who was there. It would be Peverelle. She hesitated. What if he had come in person to say he had thought matters over and had decided he neither wanted to act as her 'steady' that evening, nor marry her either?

Well, he knew what he could do, she fumed furiously. But her fury was instantly doused when she thought of her mother, her father too, waiting to meet Noah Peverelle. Oh, heavens, she'd never hear the last of it if Peverelle had called in person to tell her 'hello' and 'goodbye'.

Suddenly realising that nerves about this whole business were getting to her, Elexa made herself think more positively. Why would he come to say that he thought it a rotten idea? If they went through with it he would be getting the son he wanted. He must know by now that if he wanted some woman who wasn't out to take him to the cleaners financially, she—Alexandra Aston—was that woman.

Knowing from previous experience that he would not ring twice, Elexa picked up her bag and left her flat. Which must mean, she considered as she went down the stairs, that she herself was ready to carry this notion a little bit further. In any event, how could she now tell her mother— not to mention her aunts—that she had made up having a steady boyfriend? Oh, crumbs, another thought suddenly struck her: her mother would never forgive her if she had to pass on to her sisters, Celia and Helen, that she had a daughter who told whopping howlers!

'You needn't have rushed,' Noah Peverelle greeted her sarcastically when she at last opened the door to him.

Elexa felt inwardly agitated enough without his help, and felt very much like telling him to go find his own dinner. But memory of her mother, Aunt Celia and Aunt Helen, was recent. 'Okay, so I'll make more of an effort,' she conceded.

His grunt showed her how much he cared. 'My car's this way,' he stated. He hadn't thought better of it, then? He was still considering her 'proposition'? He touched her elbow briefly in the direction he wanted her to go, though had manners enough, she noted, to walk with her rather than go striding ahead and leaving her to trail behind. 'Where are we making for?' he asked, once they were inside his Jaguar and he had the motor purring.

'Got enough petrol for Berkshire?'

It was the last thing that was said in the car for quite some while. But the nearer they got to her parents' home, the more Elexa started to become all stewed up inside.

Until at last she just had to explode, 'This is all wrong!'

He was cool, was Peverelle; she had to give him that. If he heard the edge of panic in her voice he gave no sign. Nor, when the least she thought he might have done was to pull over and stop the car, did he do anything of the sort, but, his tone even, he enquired, 'What's wrong about it?'

'I don't know you! You don't know me!' burst from her. 'How on earth are my parents going to believe that we're an—an item?'

'Point taken,' he replied, still in that same even, unflustered way. He glanced briefly at her, but his stern expression in no way lightened when he informed her, 'I'm thirty-seven. Your friend Lois will have told you what work I do. I have a house in London and propose ultimately, perhaps when my workload lessens, to buy a place somewhere in the country.' That would please her mother. All too clearly it was pointless having a country home now, when, by the sound of it, he had no free time to spend there. 'My parents are both living in Sussex and I have a sister, Sarah, divorced and with her own home. What do I need to know about you?' He ended as if that was all he believed she needed to know—and sounded as though he wasn't too bothered whether she told him anything about herself or not.

'Have you ever been married?' Since they had got started on this, she was suddenly not ready to risk tripping up on some unexpected nugget of information he might have chosen to keep to himself.

'Never found the time,' he answered, when for a moment there she'd thought he wouldn't. 'Nor,' he added as an afterthought, 'the inclination.'

From that she gathered that he had never fallen in love with any of the women he dated. That he hadn't spent his life celibate seemed pretty obvious, without that conversation she had overheard when his friend Marcus had referred to Peverelle's women-friends. Elexa stole a sideways glance at him—and quickly away again. He had a virile sort of look about him—there was a pounding in her ears suddenly; she didn't want to think about that.

'Until now,' she said in a rush. 'You've never contemplated marriage?'

He did not answer straight away, but then—and she could only conclude he had decided that there had perhaps to be a little give and take here—he unbent sufficiently to concede, 'I've had moments recently when I've started to wonder what it's all about...'

Elexa began to like him a little. 'You mean the constant striving, being successful—but with no anchor—roots—' She broke off, a shade embarrassed. 'You spoke of buying a property in the country. I—er—thought that meant putting down roots. Somewhere for your son and heir to grow up and—' Again she broke off. She had a feeling she was getting in too deep here. She didn't want to know. She didn't want that depth of involvement. 'Anyhow,' she went on hurriedly, 'the fates may not be kind to you—it could be your child will be a girl.'

'The fates wouldn't dare,' he decreed, and for all his expression was as unsmiling as ever she saw he had a sense of humour.

Her mouth picked up at the corners. Quickly, though, she repressed any semblance of a smile. For goodness' sake—she'd be really liking him next, and that would never do. Clinical, detached; that was the way—if a way there was at all—that she wanted any 'arrangement' with him to go. The word 'detached' started to trip her up. How in creation could she be detached when…? She was glad when Noah Peverelle interrupted her thoughts.

'You're twenty-five, I believe.'

She had forgotten for the moment that he'd had her investigated. Perhaps that was why he hadn't bothered asking her questions about herself. 'I expect you know all there is to know about me,' she answered, striving hard not to sound peeved.

'I wouldn't say that,' he denied. 'I know your grandfather made his money in retail, and set your father up in business. You're an only child, by the sound of it with a doting mother who, obviously happy in her own marriage, believes that the only way her daughter will ever be as truly happy is if said daughter marries, and soon.'

'Sounds pretty ghastly, doesn't it?' Elexa had to admit.

'There are few worse fates,' he agreed solemnly. But, turning to stare at him, Elexa wasn't at all sure that she didn't catch the merest curve of movement at the corner of his excellent mouth.

Excellent? Oh, for Heaven's sake. 'Perhaps I should mention my cousin Rory's wedding,' she said hastily. 'I think my mother may bring it up. Um—I know things, mutually, may not go any further between us than this one—er—meeting, but my mother is bound to endorse the invitation to you that her sister, Rory's mother, phoned me to extend.'

'You're getting pressured by your aunt as well?' He seemed amazed.

Elexa gave him top marks for catching on so quickly. 'Aunts,' she corrected, glancing at him to see that he had noted the added pressure she was under, but going on, 'Aunt Helen, Rory's mother, rang wanting your address so she could arrange for the invitation to be mailed to you.'

Noah mentioned to Elexa the area of London where he had his house, and queried, 'If the invitations are going out, I take it the wedding is nigh?'

'Six or seven weeks,' she answered. 'But—and I can't imagine you getting pushed into a corner with no way out—if you do feel obliged to accept my mother's proxy invitation, I'll find a way of getting you out of it later.'

She looked at him—his lips had definitely twitched then. 'I think I can safely be left to manage that on my own,' he replied—and once again Elexa felt very much like hitting him.

On which pugilistic moment, they arrived in her home village. 'Turn left here,' she ordered crisply. She half expected him to turn right, just to show her that nobody bossed him around, but clearly he was made of more superior stuff than that, and steered the car left, and soon he was making another left up her parents' drive.

Her tall and slender mother was dressed in one of her smartest outfits, Elexa observed when, taking Noah into the drawing-room, she made the introductions. Her mother was a charming hostess and in no time, Elexa's father having seen to the drinks, they were all seated and in light conversation. What surprised her, though, was to see another facet of Noah Peverelle's character when he, in turn, was equally charming. Her mother was bowled over, at any rate.

Elexa watched him, ready to take up cudgels on her mother's behalf at any first sign that he might be privately having an inner laugh at her mother's expense. But studying him as she did, she saw no such hint, so that gradually, having been extremely tense at the start, Elexa began to unwind almost completely.

Almost completely, but not quite. Because when they moved from the drawing-room to the dining-room and began dinner, there were a few small snares during the meal that caused her to tense up again.

'Elexa has been very reticent in telling us about you, Noah.' Her mother smiled as she offered him more broccoli. 'I don't even know where the two of you met!'

Oh, help! Elexa wasn't good at lying, and too late realised that if she was going to lie she ought at least to have rehearsed it first. She opened her mouth to make some comment, to intercede on Noah's behalf. But then found he did not require her help. Though, whether *he* had rehearsed the lie or not, his powers of invention, instant or otherwise, were far greater than hers, she very soon realised.

'I was in one of the offices at the Samara Group when Elexa called to discuss a marketing plan with the head of department there,' he answered pleasantly.

Stunned, Elexa could only stare while her mother beamed and accepted straight away that the international chairman of that group must have taken a shine to her daughter on that instant. 'Elexa is so good at planning,' Kaye Aston told him enthusiastically. Every bit, Elexa thought in amazement, as if she stood at her elbow in her office watching her. 'In fact,' she went on, 'Elexa has always been academically quite brilliant.' While Elexa wanted to sink through the floor it was so embarrassing— her aunt Celia had used to go on like this to David about her daughter Joanna—her mother was adding, 'Academically brilliant, but so unworldly about life.'

Heaven help us, her mother was all but warning Noah to look after her prized chick! 'Aunt Helen rang!' she interrupted, saying the first thing that came to her—too late realising she had triggered off an invitation to Rory and Martina's wedding.

'She said she would.' Kaye Aston cheerfully admitted that the two of them had been under discussion. 'You will be able to come to Rory's wedding, I hope, Noah?'

'I expect Noah has a full diary,' Waldo Aston chipped in, much to Elexa's relief.

Her relief was short-lived. 'Oh, you business people,' her mother declared. 'Elexa works all hours *and* takes papers home, when there's absolutely no need for her to work at all. Yet she's never missed a day at Colman and Fisher in all the time she's been there.' She laughed lightly. 'I'm sure she'd crawl there on her hands and knees if she had to.' Elexa sent a desperate kind of look to her father, but her mother had warmed to her theme, and before he could say anything, 'Why, I remember her struggling into work one day when she was so ill she was as near to having pneumonia as—'

'A slight exaggeration,' Elexa jumped in quickly. For goodness' sake, Peverelle was a sophisticated man of the world—he didn't need to hear her mother singing her daughter's virtues—if virtues they were.

'Not at all,' Kaye Aston insisted lightly. And in friendly fashion continued, 'I swear, Noah, this daughter of mine truly believes Colman and Fisher would collapse without her.'

'Elexa is a great asset to them,' he answered smoothly, every bit as if he knew it for certain.

'What's for pudding, Mother?' Elexa asked, cringing where she sat, not bothered in the slightest about pudding, but ready to grasp at anything to change the subject.

'Gypsy tart and or cheesecake,' her mother replied, and drew breath to turn to her daughter's 'steady' again, but was forestalled when her husband, perhaps having picked up his daughter's distress signals, beat her to it.

'You don't by any chance collect stamps?' he asked Noah.

'I'm afraid I don't. It's a fascinating hobby, I've heard.'

Elexa was glad when the meal was over, and left Noah and her father in the drawing-room while she helped her mother clear the dining-room table.

'Your father and I will see to the dishes later.' Kaye Aston beamed. And, because it seemed she just couldn't resist it, she declared, 'Oh, darling, if I'd chosen someone for you myself I couldn't have chosen better.'

Elexa stared at her parent and couldn't help feeling slightly staggered. Only a week ago her mother had been all for her being 'nice' to Tommy Fielding. Noah Peverelle and Tommy Fielding weren't in the same street! 'Er— we're only dating,' she thought she had better mention. She had no idea yet which way this arrangement, or non-arrangement, was going.

'You told Tommy Fielding you were seeing someone, long-term. Oh, please don't tell me you're thinking of just moving in with him.'

'I can promise you, Mum, that's the last thing I'm think-ing of,' Elexa replied, glad to be able to be honest about that at least. While she owned to starting to feel more than

a touch confused about what she was doing—she could
hardly imagine she'd had the nerve to ring Peverelle the
way she had last Sunday—she was clear about that. She
had her own place—why would she want to move into
his?

Her mother seemed so relieved she came and gave her
a hug, 'You will tell me—as soon as there is anything to
tell me?' she asked urgently.

She meant an engagement, or marriage, Elexa knew that
she did, and as her heart went all soft on her Elexa forgot
for the moment the weight of pressure—well-meaning, but
pressure all the same—that her parents constantly applied
in their urgency for her to be married. All Elexa knew then
was that she loved her worrying mother, and that if it
would mean so very much to her to see her walk down
that aisle then, if Peverelle was willing, it didn't seem such
a huge step to take.

'I'll be on the phone to you as soon as,' she promised.

But when, not long afterwards, she was seated beside
Peverelle as he drove them back to London she was starting to have second thoughts, and that wedding aisle
seemed suddenly ten miles long.

Barely a word passed between them on the return jour-
ney, which was all right by Elexa; she had a lot on her
mind. She guessed that Noah Peverelle had too, because
they had almost arrived at her door before he let her into
some of his thoughts.

'It's a bit late for us to have any lengthy discussion—
there are things I have to ask you, matters you'll want to
clear up with me,' he said. 'I'll give you a call in the
morning and arrange a time to talk the whole situation
through.'

Elexa swallowed. He hadn't met the chief members of
her family and rejected the notion out of hand, then? She

began to feel a bit shaky inside. Now, she realised, was the time to tell him that she'd changed her mind, that she didn't want to take it any further.

Against that, though, was the certainty that her mother would be twice as protective of her if she thought that she was broken-hearted that she had split with her 'steady'.

Noah Peverelle pulled the Jaguar up outside of her apartment building and Elexa knew she had to tell him something—either, yes, give me a call, or, no, don't bother. She turned to look at him, thinking over what he had just said. Solemnly he stared back at her. Her heart picked up a panicky beat.

Then suddenly she recalled he had included her viewpoint in his 'matters you'll want to clear up with me' and she began to like him a little more. No way could she accuse him of looking at everything from purely his own angle.

'Fine,' she agreed at last, and still feeling shaky she got out of the car.

Noah got out of the car too, and went to the outer door with her, but waited only long enough for her to find her key and unlock the door. Then, 'Goodnight,' he said brusquely—and went back to his car.

He was driving away before she had the door closed, and, alone once more, Elexa immediately began to have doubts. She had just spent several hours with him, but she was no nearer to knowing the man. She did not know him. In fact, the man was a stranger to her. Was she honestly, truly, thinking of marrying him?

CHAPTER THREE

WITH the coming of daylight the doubts and fears of her night-time thoughts seemed to lessen, and Elexa began to realise that perhaps it might be better if she didn't know Noah Peverelle. Wouldn't it be better if the man remained a stranger? Well, not a complete stranger, of course, but she didn't have to dwell on that.

The ringing of the telephone brought her from her bed, and at her initial thought that it might be him she felt all fluttery inside. But she need not have worried; it was not Noah Peverelle—it was her mother. She should have known!

'I'm sorry to ring so early,' Kaye Aston chirruped excitedly. She was sorry—so early—this was new! 'Dawn patrol, your father calls me—but I know you're an early riser too,' she burbled on. 'The thing is, I just had to ring to say how much your father and I took to Noah. Oh, he's such a charming man. I'm going to call Celia and Helen in a minute, and—'

'*Mother!*'

'Yes, I know, I know. You're only dating him at the moment and it's nothing more than that. But you've never gone steady with any man before, so it will be,' her mother stated, so totally convinced that Elexa didn't have a chance of persuading her otherwise. 'Now, tell me. When are you seeing him again?'

'I'm not,' Elexa replied.

'You mean you haven't arranged a date. Now, isn't that what I've just been saying? The two of you are so "right" with each other that you don't have to make arrangements any more. Noah just pops round to see you as much as he possibly can. And I expect you're forever talking to each other on the phone while he's away.' Kaye Aston paused to take a breath, and Elexa managed to get a word in.

'He's going to ring me this morning,' she volunteered, wondering as she said it if she wouldn't be wiser—instead of perpetuating this myth that she was dating someone—if she hinted they were on the brink of a mutual falling-out.

'There!' Kaye Aston sighed, which meant, Elexa supposed, that it was just as her mother had thought. 'Noah could be trying to get you right this minute!' she suddenly exclaimed. 'I'll go. I won't ring you again today—don't want to intrude if you have Noah with you. I'll ring you tomorrow.'

Elexa just had time to thank her for the very nice meal she had arranged for them last night, then her mother said goodbye. Elexa put the phone down, realising that was the second of her parent's shorter calls in two days. And, although she was on the receiving end of pressure of a different sort, it seemed that just by having a 'steady' the pressure of long and lengthy phone calls was already letting up.

When Noah Peverelle telephoned a couple of hours later Elexa was looking on him a little more favourably than she had. For a start she knew that the earliest her mother was going to make contact again would be tomorrow morning.

'I'm free to come round now,' he suggested without preamble.

Elexa's stomach did an unexpected somersault. She had thought when he'd said he would arrange a time to talk the whole situation through that it would be perhaps next week some time, or maybe the week after. 'I'll put some coffee on,' she replied, outwardly calm.

'I'll be with you in half an hour.' The line went dead and Elexa swallowed hard, and felt hot all over. Suddenly she couldn't think of one solitary matter that she wanted to clear up with him.

She felt anxious and nervy all at once, and went swiftly to her bedroom to check her appearance. She was normally smart; it was the way she had been brought up. Looking at her reflection in her full-length mirror, she saw that there did not seem too much wrong with her appearance. Fine wool tailored trousers neatly covered her long legs and slender lower half, and the cream sweater that hinted at the shapely curves of her upper half went well with her long blonde hair with its hint of pale gold. She wore little make-up, but the touch of lipstick to her mouth enhanced its full sweetness. The large brown eyes that stared back at her as she raised her glance up from her mouth and past her dainty nose showed perhaps just a hint of the inner agitation she was feeling.

She ran a comb through her hair and left it loose, down to halfway between her shoulderblades. She spent the rest of the time while waiting attempting to assemble together everything she wanted to ask, or thought maybe she should ask Noah Peverelle when he arrived.

Elexa also made every effort to clam up her agitated feelings. For Heaven's sake, she had a reputation at the office for being absolutely unflappable—grief, hurry up and get some professionalism going!

By the time the half-hour was up she thought she had succeeded. But, even when she was expecting Noah to buzz up at any moment, she jumped nervously when the buzzer went. 'Hello?' she enquired calmly into the intercom. It would be him. But who knew? It could have been somebody else.

'Peverelle,' he answered.

Without saying a word she released the outer door catch and spent the short time remaining endeavouring to hang on to a feeling of being in control.

'Come in,' she smiled when she opened her door to the tall, good-looking man standing there. This morning Peverelle's long length was clad in casual trousers, shirt and light sweater. He did not smile in return. 'I'll pour that coffee,' she said, taking him into her sitting-room, but needing a moment or two alone to calm herself. She had thought she had herself under control. But this man was unnerving. Not to mention the reason why he was here.

He took his coffee black without sugar, and, having handed him his, and taken hers to the chair facing the one he occupied, Elexa thought that the sooner they began the sooner she might start to feel less on edge.

She took the metaphorical bull by the horns and dived in. 'Y-you said there were things you wanted to ask me.'

Noah Peverelle stared at her with that long stern look she was growing familiar with. 'I make you nervous?' he enquired coolly, and Elexa started to dislike him again. She had thought her nervousness hidden, but trust him to notice.

'This isn't an everyday situation,' she answered bluntly, a touch aggressively, she had to admit.

Again came that stern look. Then, surprisingly, he gave her the benefit of a hint of a smile. 'I wouldn't argue that,' he replied—and Elexa ditched her dislike of him. 'We've had chance now to spend a few hours in each other's company,' he went on. 'Time enough, I believe, for both of us to know if either of us have been totally put off the idea of going through a marriage ceremony with the other.' So *that* was why he had gone with her to her parents' last evening. *That*, perhaps, more than to check out the main members of her family for himself.

'Do I take it that by being here at all you haven't yet gone off the idea?' she asked.

'You are as brilliant academically as your mother said you were,' he replied. Was he being sarcastic? Before Elexa could do more then bridle, however, he was asking, 'You agreed to my coming here this morning. Do I take it you haven't gone off the idea either?'

'It's not something I want to undertake lightly,' she answered. 'But already my mother's telephone calls seem to be shorter. I love to hear from her,' she added quickly. 'It's…'

'Just that you're finding it more and more difficult to put up with that one topic of conversation grinding you down,' he finished for her.

'That's about it. I don't need it—just,' she inserted, 'as I don't need marriage—on her terms. I love my job; I'm good at it. There's a junior manager's job becoming vacant in the not too distant future,' she confided. 'I know I'm good enough to do that job.'

'How would you cope with your job *and* pregnancy?' Noah asked—he could have been talking over any other business for all the emotion she could detect in his voice.

'That wouldn't be a problem,' she answered. 'I've some holiday entitlement from this year that I can carry over until next year. That, with next year's holiday allowance, means that I can take my holiday for—er—any—um—confinement, without having to draw on any statutory maternity leave. I wouldn't want to be away from the office for too long anyhow, especially if I get the junior manager position.'

Noah took that on board, and asked, 'You're in good health?'

She stared at him. He had a stern expression again as he studied her. 'Extremely,' she answered. He'd be wanting to examine her teeth next! 'You heard my mother. I've never had a day off work through illness in my working career.'

'You're more interested in your career than in marriage?'

She'd thought that was already established. But if he needed her to endorse it, so be it. 'I always have been— career minded, that is. To be completely honest with you—'

'It's the only way for us to be with each other if this venture is to have any success,' he chipped in.

'Well, then,' she continued, 'I've never before given marriage any thought because, well, truthfully, I've never fancied anyone all that much. I'm twenty-five,' she went on, telling him what she knew he already knew, 'and I don't think I ever will. So the probability is that, in the more normal way of doing things, I shall stay happy in my career, but unmarried. But, as I believe I mentioned, I don't think I should like to wake up one morning to realise I should like a child, only to discover I have left it too late.'

Noah Peverelle thought about that for a moment or two and then, with that direct kind of look she was beginning to associate with him, 'You don't have any objection to me having the child living with me?'

Logically, it went without saying that any child of his would have the best nanny to be found, and Elexa knew that any child they produced between them would be much better off with him. She had her career. Peverelle already had plans to buy somewhere out in the country.

'You'd grant me access, of course?' she questioned, knowing suddenly, without having to think about it, that, career or no career having to come first, there was no way she would be able to give birth to some little mite and then completely forget him.

The man opposite studied her, his glance raking down to the slight, but determined, jutting of her jaw. 'I suppose I should have thought of that,' he replied at length. Then conceded, 'Perhaps it would be better for the child to know you.' Suddenly, though, that stern expression was back. 'You're fully aware that I'm not interested in any long-term relationship?'

'Don't flatter yourself!' she erupted. 'Were it not for my family, I wouldn't marry at all.'

'Your mother would just love that—you having a child out of wedlock.'

That surprised her—that Peverelle had seen her mother just once and had known straight away that she would be absolutely appalled should her daughter produce a child without being married. Though perhaps it shouldn't have surprised her; he had known in advance that her mother was desperate for her to find a husband.

She sighed. 'I suppose if I'm not to leave myself open for more trouble, it has to be marriage.'

'I wouldn't consider the other option,' he stated forcefully.

This time Elexa stared at him, her brown eyes wide. It was common enough these days for children to be born without benefit of their parents going through a marriage ceremony. She wouldn't have thought it would matter to him either way, so long as he had the son he wanted. Curiosity would out. 'Why?' she just had to ask.

He shrugged, but made no bones about telling her.

'When the time comes I want my rights to the child firmly established.'

Elexa wasn't with him for a moment, but then all at once it clicked, and she stared at him open-mouthed. 'You need this marriage so that in the event I decide "thank you very much, but I've decided to keep any—um—baby" you'd have as much legal right as me?' she asked sharply.

'I prefer to eliminate all risks before we start.'

'You don't trust me?' she flared, feeling quite annoyed.

'I don't know you,' he clipped shortly.

Elexa was ready to flare up at him again, but then realised that he was quite right. He didn't know her any more than she knew him. They were two strangers, each with a mutual need of the other—on a temporary basis only.

'A necessary evil,' she commented, and saw his lips twitch. It made him more human somehow.

'For both of us,' he answered. But, as if he wanted to keep this discussion as businesslike as possible, given the circumstances, 'I'll get my lawyers to—'

'Lawyers!' she butted in. 'I don't want any lawyers knowing anything about our arrangement! There's no need for anyone else to know about any—er—decision we come to but our two selves.' Grief, some lawyers—and probably the firm he would use—were vast organisations. She could see now everyone down to the lowest paid discussing all their business.

'We'll need lawyers for the divorce, and, of course, for your settlement.'

'Settlement!' she exclaimed, staring at him horror struck.

'Naturally you'll want a financial—'

'I don't want your money!' she exploded before he could finish. 'I'm quite aware just how much you love money-grubbing females. How dare you put me in the same category as…?' she stopped, and took a deep and controlling breath. 'I'm being cantankerous again, aren't I?'

He smiled then. For the first time since she had known him, he smiled, and it did wonderful things to him. His whole expression seemed to lighten, and Elexa wasn't sure that her heart didn't give a little flutter.

She was discounting any such ridiculous notion a moment later. But by then Noah was stating, 'You're nervous, and I've offended you. I apologise for that, but I believed it would be better to get everything cleared up before I went away and left you to think everything through—before you decide if you want to go through with this.'

Her heart definitely did flutter then. 'Does that mean you've already decided what it is *you* want to do?'

He looked at her levelly, his grey eyes fixed on her, holding her eyes, refusing to let her look away. 'I want a son,' he stated. 'I would prefer not to marry, but, since I need to protect my parental rights, I'm prepared to make a temporary marriage. You have reasons too for wanting a marriage certificate. A brief marriage to each other would, I believe, suit us both.'

Elexa swallowed. There it was. Noah Peverelle had just offered to marry her. She felt all shaky inside. She wasn't ready to say yes; she knew that she wasn't. 'Y-you mentioned giving me time to think everything through…'

'I'll be out of town from now until Thursday afternoon,' he replied. 'If you've anything to tell me, give me a ring on Thursday evening.'

If she hadn't anything to tell him, then she could forget it, she realised, and was angry with herself that she felt quite miffed that it obviously didn't matter to him too much whether she said yes or no.

He was already getting to his feet, prepared to leave,

when he asked, 'If there's nothing further you want to know?'

'I wouldn't have to live with you?' she blurted out, on her feet too.

He looked down at her, his glance going over her pale gold-lit head, when to her astonishment, he stated, 'Beautiful though you undoubtedly are, Elexa, I'd prefer that you didn't.'

She wanted to swallow again, it momentarily passing her by that he had no time for that sort of domesticity. He thought her beautiful! Quickly, though, she got herself together. If they weren't going to live together—and Heaven forbid that should ever happen, even temporarily—then how…?

'Er…' She felt herself blushing, and she hadn't asked the question yet!

He looked mildly surprised at the sudden pink tinge to her skin. 'You're uncomfortable about something?' he asked, as ever coming straight to the point. 'Huh.' He sifted and found the problem himself. 'You're wondering about, for the want of a better phrase, the sleeping arrangements?'

Pink turned to red—even her ears felt on fire. 'W-would we have to—um—have any—er—contact?' she questioned. And, in a rush, 'Th-there are scientific ways now, I think, that…' She didn't get to finish, though she doubted that it was to spare her blushes that Noah Peverelle was soon chopping her off.

'I would prefer natural to scientific for my son.'

She was stumped to answer that. 'Oh,' she murmured feebly.

'You're numerate; you'd have to be in your job,' he commented. 'Should we marry, I'd leave you to contact me when you've calculated your fertile period. The time when you are most likely to conceive,' he endorsed, and turned to leave.

Elexa was still trying to credit that she had actually had this conversation, when Noah Peverelle paused and then turned back to face her. When he stood, just surveying her for a moment or two, she somehow knew she wasn't going to like what was coming, whatever it was.

She was right—he hadn't yet done with matters intimate, it seemed. 'Your mother seems to believe that you're a touch unworldly, so I hope you'll forgive me for being a shade indelicate,' he began. 'But if you and I are to indulge in unprotected—involvement, I think it's necessary for me to know—have you had many partners?'

Heavens above! 'N-no,' she stammered. 'Er—nothing you need be concerned over.' She was dying a death here. But, in an endeavour that he shouldn't know it, 'How about you?' she asked the tall virile-looking man.

'I've had my moments, naturally,' he answered, not a blush about him. 'But you'd be safe with me. I can promise you that.'

'Good,' she said, finding the wool of his sweater of much interest. 'Then neither of us has anything to worry about.'

'If there's nothing else?' he enquired, already turning to leave.

She went with him to the door. 'Goodbye,' she bade him, and returned to her sitting-room to collapse into a chair. Worry about? Nothing to worry about?

In the following few days, in between working hard and daily telephone conversations with her mother, Elexa did nothing but worry. She spent sleepless nights worrying. Was she really contemplating marrying Noah Peverelle? Had she, in fact, actually made that initial approach to him that had started this whole thing off?

Did she want to go through with it? Did she want to make that phone call on Thursday? Her mother's telephone calls said she did. For while it was a tremendous relief that her dear parent had stepped off the 'now-here's-a-nice-man-I-want-you-to-meet' trail, her telephone calls were just as regular, only now they were full of Noah Peverelle and how Aunt Celia and Aunt Helen were just dying to meet him. So that Elexa now realised she had changed one pressure for another. Though it had to be said, she qualified, the pressure of her mother's relentless phone calls when Noah Peverelle was her theme was a vast improvement from the relentless onslaught she'd had to endure with regard to the 'nice' marriage-material males her mother seemed to have an endless supply of.

Elexa made a point of leaving work earlier than was usual on Thursday. She had done nothing but think since Noah had gone from her flat on Sunday. But with every moment getting closer to the time when she should ring him—if she was going to—she knew that she had to think that little bit harder.

She made herself a pot of tea as soon as she arrived home, and sat down to concentrate hard on what it was she wanted. The tea went cold as she tried to think logically, unemotionally, and took everything apart.

What did she want? She wanted her career. She had a super job, worked with super people, and knew she was tipped to be a high-flyer in the large concern she worked for. Her job involved planning; she was good at planning. She didn't think she was particularly maternal, but, bearing in mind how squashy she'd felt inside when nursing her cousin's baby, it seemed logical if she could plan her career for those plans to include a baby—that way she would not wake up one morning with a sudden urge to have a child only to find that her biological clock was sticking its tongue out.

In truth there was no one she fancied to be the father of her child, but with Noah Peverelle she had the guarantee that he did not want any kind of emotional involvement. Once the deed was done, it would be a race to see which one of them got to the divorce lawyer quicker. A slight snag there in that she had a vague notion that a couple had to be married for a whole year before they could divorce—but that of course didn't mean that they had to wait to set the wheels in motion.

On the other hand, perhaps it wasn't such a snag. Hadn't she thought at the start that a year free of that unremitting pressure from her mother was all she craved?

What it all boiled down to was the fact that, while she loved her family dearly, she was getting more and more worn down by them. She wanted peace to get on with her life and in her own way. She didn't want her mother, her aunts, colluding with each other on what *they* thought was right for her. They wanted her married. She could marry—but to a man of *her* choice. A man who was as keen to divorce as she was.

Noah Peverelle, in the circumstances that prevailed, was the ideal candidate. She panicked a little at the thought of having to sleep with him, but realised she could hardly complain. Recalling his suggestion that he'd leave it to her to contact him at her fertile period, he wasn't exactly champing at the bit to sleep with her either, was he?

Her eyes went to the phone. Do it, urged the logic of her head. She resisted. There was a child to consider here. Though what exactly was there to consider? If Noah Peverelle was so keen to have a son that he was prepared to give up his bachelorhood, albeit briefly, then from what she knew of him, had gleaned of him and his integrity, she had an idea that any child would be much cared for. It wasn't as if she wouldn't have access. Noah might have chief guardianship, but she felt certain, having heard his talk of it being better for the child to know her, that she would have all the access she wanted.

Having thought everything through for a final time, Elexa, though admittedly not without quite some feelings of apprehension, reached for the phone. It barely rang before it was answered.

'Peverelle,' he said firmly.

She wasn't ready. Even then, having thought about everything so much, she wasn't yet ready. 'H-hello,' she said huskily—and couldn't even get her name out to tell him who was calling.

But then she found that she did not have to. Noah Peverelle, as tintack-sharp as ever, knew with that one word who was calling. 'Does the fact that you've made this call at all mean that I can go ahead and book the registrar?' he enquired evenly.

No, Hello Elexa, how have you been. Just straight down to business, she fumed, and was glad to feel niggled; it put paid to her speechlessness. 'The baby,' she said bluntly. 'With you being so busy all the time, when are you going to have chance to be a father to him?'

'The earliest I need be around for him is in ten months' time,' Noah answered straight away, making her realise that she wasn't the only one who had thought everything through. 'While the child is an infant I'll see him at every available opportunity. I'm already aiming to lessen my workload. All being well, give it a couple of years and I shall be in a position to enjoy both him and that place in the country I spoke of.' He let that sink in, then asked seriously, 'Anything else bothering you?'

'Um—wh-where do I tell people I met you?' she asked,

realising as the question left her lips that she had more or less agreed that he could book the register office, and that she was just clutching at last minute panicky straws.

'You mean Lois Crosby?'

Was he sharp, or was he sharp? 'I suppose so,' Elexa answered—her parents already believed they had met when Noah had seen her at one of his offices. 'Lois was the person I rang when I wanted your home number.' Elexa supposed he already knew that, just as he seemed to know that she hadn't told Lois *why* she wanted his home number.

'You don't feel like telling her you wanted my number because you found me so fascinating you just had to contact me to ask me for a date?'

He was teasing. Wasn't he? Elexa realised she didn't know him well enough to be sure. 'Lois doesn't believe in fairy stories,' Elexa answered crisply, and knew the tension she had been under this last few days must have got to her when she actually thought she heard the stern-expressioned man she knew give a smothered laugh. She didn't believe she had amused him for a minute.

And was right not to believe it, she realised a moment later when, quite soberly, he suggested, 'Did you perhaps need my home number to try the personal touch when Colman and Fisher were trying a new marketing approach?'

'Oh, I did!' Elexa accepted gratefully, ignoring that that type of work wasn't anything to do with her section. 'I don't want to lie to Lois, but I'd prefer no one but just you and I know of our—arrangement.'

'Do I take it from that that you and I are—engaged?'

'We needn't go overboard!' Elexa, answered sharply. But then had to laugh. 'That was a bit crass wasn't it?'

'Accepting to marry me, but not to be engaged?'

'I—um—have accepted, haven't I?'

'I rather think you have,' Noah replied, going on in a businesslike way, 'We might as well do it straight away. Any objections to a special licence? We could be married next week and...'

'Why the rush?' She cut him off. He was going too fast—she needed time, time for it to settle more firmly in her mind that she had just agreed to marry him.

'Why would you want to wait?' he countered. 'The sooner we marry, the sooner we can get the divorce underway,' he stated crisply.

It wasn't the most romantic proposal she had ever heard. But she brought herself up short. For Heaven's sake, who wanted romance? 'I don't care when,' she answered, striving hard to be as businesslike as him, 'but my mother might be a touch scandalised if I do her out of the white wedding bit.'

'You have to tell her?'

'You're suggesting we marry first and tell her *afterwards*?' she questioned astonished. 'I couldn't do that to her!'

There was a short silence, then Noah, ever the decision-maker, was informing her, 'I'm fairly tied up the week after next. I could manage Tuesday of the following week.'

'I'd prefer not to lose a day off work. Could you make a Saturday or a Sunday?'

'I'll have to check my office and get back to you,' he answered, and asked, 'You don't want me to call on your father or any of that stuff, do you?'

To ask for her hand? 'Grief, no!' she exclaimed, everything seeming to be going along at too fast a pace all of a sudden. 'There's no need for that. It's not as if—' She broke off, suddenly horrified to feel emotional tears catch her throat. Get a grip, for goodness' sake. Hadn't she already tossed romance and all that sort of nonsense in the bin? 'Shall I ring and tell my parents?' she asked briskly.

'It will make your mother's day,' he suggested nicely. Swine! 'Anything you need to ask? Discuss?' he asked.

'Not a thing,' she replied.

'I'll be in touch.'

This was her call. 'Goodnight,' she bade him, and quickly put down the phone. She'd done it! She had promised to marry a man who was virtually a stranger! Her mouth went dry and she felt all of a tremble inside. She sank back in her chair, musing a shade shakily that it seemed an enormous step to take—and yet, at the same time, it also seemed oddly the right thing to do.

Elexa was still mulling over the peculiarity of that when suddenly her phone rang. She jumped, her thoughts flying to Noah, the man she had just agreed to marry. Was he calling back to discuss something he had overlooked? Her heartbeat crazily seemed to speed up. She made herself calm down. Of course it wouldn't be him! As if Noah Peverelle would forget anything!

It wasn't Noah—it was her mother. 'Is it tonight that Noah comes back?' she enquired.

Elexa knew her mother knew full well that Noah was returning from his business trip that day, because her mother had mentioned it on every phone call since Monday. 'He's home,' Elexa answered.

'Oh, lovely. You'll be longing to see him, I expect?'

Tell her. The words got stuck. It was as if once she had told her parent that she and Noah were going to be married she was committed. **'Actually, Mum...'** she began hesitantly.

'What's happened?'

'Nothing. Well, that is. Um...' Elexa took a deep breath. 'Actually,' she plunged, 'Noah and I are getting married.'

And quickly pulled the phone away from her ear at her mother's ear-piercing scream of joy.

There followed a few minutes of split sentences, her mother pretending she wasn't in tears, and Elexa having burning coals of guilt raining down on her because she was deceiving her parent so.

'Celia and Helen will be delighted,' Kaye Aston crooned, and Elexa knew that the phone lines from her parents' home would be buzzing the moment she had said goodbye to her. 'Have you got your engagement ring yet? Oh, I'm just dying to see it,' her mother rushed on. 'Have you decided when the wedding will be? I always think a June wedding is lovely. We'll have to—'

'Noah,' Elexa cut in, 'and I,' she added quickly, 'were thinking of sooner than that.' June was next year! Hang it, they'd be closer to divorce than to getting married by then!

'Sooner? How much sooner? They'll be a lot to arrange, Elexa.'

'Actually, we thought we'd marry in about—er—three weeks' time,' Elexa answered—and held the phone away from her ear for a second time.

'Three weeks!' her mother shrieked, and Elexa thought she had better let her have the rest of it now rather than later.

'Noah's going to check the date. You know how busy he is. It will probably be a Saturday, if the—um—r-registrar can...'

Elexa was sitting stunned five minutes later, feeling she had just been pulled well and truly through the wringer. When the phone rang again she felt very much like not answering it. For certain it was going to be either her mother or one of her aunts.

She stretched out a hand to the instrument, knowing without a question of doubt that should she not answer it, her mother would ring every fifteen minutes until she did. 'Hello,' she said, perhaps a shade warily—and discovered it was none of her female relatives.

'Something wrong?' Noah asked.

'Oh, it's you,' Elexa answered in relief. But only for that relief to rapidly subside when she thought of what she had to tell him.

'You thought it would be someone else? Your mother?' he guessed.

'I've just been speaking to her. Correction, my mother has just been speaking to me, rather severely.'

'Snap!' he answered.

Elexa's eyes shot wide. 'My mother rang *you*!' she gasped, hardly able to believe it.

'Not your mother, my mother. I thought while she was on that I might as well tell her I was getting married.'

'She didn't like it?' Elexa guessed—he'd intimated his parent had spoken to him severely.

'She loved it. She wants to meet you.'

'Oh, no!' Elexa exclaimed instinctively. 'What excuse did you make?' she asked, knowing for sure he would have got them out of it.

'I didn't,' he replied coolly. 'Once my mother knew I had met your parents, I was sunk.' His mother sounded as forceful as hers. 'How does dinner in Sussex next Tuesday suit you?'

It didn't. 'How does a church wedding, choir, church bells and all my relations attending suit you?' she responded.

'The Register Office deal is off?'

'My mother went ballistic at that one.'

'Can she do it all in three weeks? From what I've gathered, these things are a year in the planning.'

'You don't know my mother. Er—does that mean—

you're agreeable—to a church wedding? Me in the white frock?'

His reply shattered her. 'I'm sure you'll look lovely,' he said. Her mouth fell open—this, from that stern man she knew! But, once more businesslike, he was going on, 'I'd better have the name of the church and the minister.'

Elexa named the church in her home village, though thought if he intended to ring the vicar that night then he might have to wait to get through—her mother was probably on to the vicar right at this minute.

'I'll call for you around six on Tuesday,' her intended informed her. 'You'd better come and have a look at my place before we go—it will obviate any questioning glances if it appears you've never seen the inside of where I live.'

'Fine,' she answered, and said goodbye feeling mightily relieved that he had taken her mother's insistence on a church wedding so well.

On Saturday she and Lois went shopping for a wedding dress. Joanna and Lois were to be her attendants, and had arranged to shop for their dresses the following Saturday.

Lois accepted totally without question that Elexa had met Noah after telephoning him about business, and exclaimed that it must have been love at first or second sight for both of them.

'It all happened very quickly,' Elexa said, which—leaving out the 'love' bit—she supposed it had.

'I'll say it was quick,' Lois surmised lightly. 'He hasn't had time yet to get you an engagement ring.'

Elexa made a mental note to buy herself a ring—her mother would want to see one the next time they met.

In the circumstances, and her own taste being more to the classic than the frothy, Elexa did not want anything too elaborate in the way of a wedding dress. So she could only suppose it must have been some of Lois's enthusiasm rubbing off that she allowed herself to be persuaded to try on a rather beautiful creation of chiffon and lace.

'You look fantastic!' Lois whispered, and was almost in tears. 'You've got to have it, Elexa. You just have to.'

Elexa, not having wanted to have a white wedding at all, looked at her reflection in the full-length mirror, and—strangely at that point a picture of Noah Peverelle coming into her head—answered, 'I think I shall.'

Tuesday came around before she was ready for it. She went into work an hour early so that she could leave early to get ready to go to meet Noah's parents. She owned to feeling extremely apprehensive about the meeting, and hoped with all she had that they would not ask anything of her that called for an outright lie.

Noah was on time, but she saw no sense in inviting him up only for him to have to go down again. 'I'm on my way,' she said into the intercom, and her heart was feeling a touch fluttery at the prospect of seeing him again—quite normal, she would have thought, given she was going to marry him yet barely knew him.

He was as good-looking as ever, she saw as she opened the door and joined him. 'How have the phone calls been?' he asked pleasantly as they made their way to his car.

She knew he was meaning from her mother. 'Quite good,' she answered with a smile. 'I rather think my mother believes she has to do her best to keep me calm before the "big day".'

As Noah had suggested, they stopped off first at his gracious town house. 'Come on in,' he invited, and showed her over the elegantly but comfortably furnished drawing-room, breakfast room, his study and a few of the other rooms before turning to escort her out to his car. They were still in the hall though when he halted her. 'Just a minute,' And so, saying, he handed her a small square box.

'What is it?'

'Your engagement ring—my mother wanted details,' he explained.

'So did mine,' Elexa commented. 'I was going to buy one,' she said, and asked, 'How much do I owe you?'

He looked slightly startled. 'For what?'

'The ring,' she answered, and, looking up into his face, she saw a kind of smile pass over his features.

'Now are you a one,' he murmured, and Elexa felt all kind of funny inside.

Quickly she looked down. She was holding the small box. She opened it, and the most gorgeous diamond solitaire winked up at her. 'Is it real?' she gasped.

'Would I give you paste?' he replied.

She looked up at him again, aware that had he accepted payment for the ring she would have had to dig quite deeply into her financial assets. 'I'll let you have it back,' she said. 'When this is all over, I'll return it to you.'

He stared at her. 'You truly are something else again,' he commented, shaking his head. 'Put it on,' he suggested, 'and let's get down to Sussex.'

The engagement ring was starting to feel less strange on her engagement finger by the time they reached his parents' large old house.

Elexa, while not outwardly showing it, felt highly nervous. She also felt extremely guilty when Ruth and Brandon Peverelle warmly welcomed her and said how delighted they had been to hear Noah's news.

Over dinner Ruth Peverelle spoke of relatives and a few friends who would like to attend the wedding, and Elexa passed on her mother's request to let her have any names and addresses, so she could send them a wedding invitation.

'Your poor mother,' Ruth Peverelle sympathised. 'It wasn't very kind of you, Noah, to drop the wedding on her at such short notice.'

'Neither Elexa nor I want to wait,' Noah answered his mother, and Elexa felt more guilt. Mrs Peverelle's gentle expression said only too clearly that she thought her son and his future bride were desperately in love with each other.

Elexa was grateful to Noah that he took the conversation away from talk of the wedding and conversed with his father on matters concerning his father's seeming hobby of taking engines apart and putting them back together again.

Though she guessed that Noah must be tuned in to whatever was going on around him. Because when his mother turned to her and stumped her with the question, 'I expect you'll be moving into Noah's house once you are married?' it was Noah who broke off from what he was saying to his father, to reply for her.

'Elexa has her own apartment. With me being away so much, and with Elexa's flat so convenient to her place of work, it seems best to float between our two homes. Meantime, I shall be looking for somewhere to buy in the country.'

Elexa had to admire him, she really did. If he managed his business life as efficiently, it was no wonder he was the international chairman of the Samara Group. For—apart from 'floating between their two homes'—he had answered his mother's question without having to lie. Nor perhaps, on reflection, was floating, a fib. Because when the time came, he was either going to have to float over to her place, or she was going to have to float over to his. But—she didn't want to think about that.

Elexa thought Noah's parents were lovely, but nonetheless it had been a bit of an ordeal sitting there hoping against hope that she wouldn't be called upon to tell a lie. So she was quite glad when Noah announced that they both had work to do the next day, and they said goodbye, and headed back to London.

'I'm off to the States in the morning,' Noah thought to tell her when he dropped her off at her apartment building. 'I don't know much about these things but, should you have any problems, give my PA a ring. Gillian Owen will be pleased to help and will know where to contact me.'

'I can't think there'll be any problem, but you never know,' Elexa answered. 'Have a good trip,' she wished him. 'Goodnight.'

'Goodnight,' he said quietly.

Elexa realised that there was nothing more to say. She looked up at him, his unsmiling expression illuminated in the overhead globe of the porch. Silently he stared down at her and for no reason her heart started to thunder.

She turned abruptly away and was vaguely aware of him making his way back to his car. Hurriedly she went indoors.

She climbed the stairs in something of a daze, the feel of his engagement ring on her finger proof—if proof she needed—that she had actually promised to marry Noah. But he had just gone. She had just said goodbye to him and, for all she knew, the next time she might see him would be when they stood before the minister who would make them man and wife.

She didn't know what was the matter with her, but suddenly she was feeling jumpy and illogical, which wasn't at all like her. For crying out loud, Noah Peverelle wanted no emotional entanglements, and neither did she—so why, suddenly, was she feeling so emotionally all over the place?

CHAPTER FOUR

ELEXA did not have to ring Gillian Owen because on Friday evening, eight days before the wedding, her mother phoned declaring her opinion that she and Elexa's father should meet Noah's parents before the big day and, Noah also rang—from New York.

Elexa, who hadn't heard a word from him since that visit to his parents ten days ago, and was certain he had no need to phone, had to admit that she was pleased to hear him. Though she put that down to the fact that it saved her having to ring his PA.

'Anything happening I should know about?' he asked, his tone cool.

'Um, not much. Though since you might, or might not,' she inserted hastily, 'have need to contact me, I shall be at my parents' home next Friday evening.' Her mother had insisted on that, rather than on Elexa driving herself over on Saturday morning, her wedding day.

'Anything else?' he questioned, still in that same cool tone that was starting to annoy her.

'Well, since you ask, my parents—my mother, actually—feel that they should get together with your parents before the wedding,' she answered, matching his cool tone. 'I think it's a kind of courtesy thing so that your parents don't feel left out.'

'Your mother thinks of everything,' he murmured blandly. Tell me about it! 'How does dinner next Thursday sound?'

Two days before their marriage? 'Fine,' she answered.

'Leave it with me. I'll fix it,' he said, and rang off.

Elexa owned to feeling peeved, but told herself it was nothing to do with him putting down his phone so abruptly. It was just that she was used to making decisions, to fixing things. Besides, she was there on the spot—he was in the States.

She was over her niggle of annoyance by the time Thursday arrived. Noah hadn't telephoned again, but his PA had. 'Mr Peverelle asked me to pass on details of the restaurant booking,' Gillian had begun as soon as they had made contact. She'd gone on to say that Mr Peverelle suggested, because he would be flying in that day and could be delayed, he would meet her at the restaurant. Having passed that information on, she had relaxed sufficiently to say, 'His work schedule is crazy, but as usual he'll get through it.' And she added, 'May I wish you all the very best for your wedding?'

Elexa had thought that was very sweet of her, thanked her, and had rung her mother to acquaint her with the details.

As arranged, her parents having no idea where the Falcon Restaurant was, they called for her on Thursday so she should show them the way. 'You'll be longing to see Noah,' her mother commented when the three of them were in Waldo Aston's car.

'Of course.' Elexa smiled, but could not in all honesty have said what she was feeling.

What she did know, however, was that her equilibrium was mightily upset when, as she and her parents stepped into the restaurant—Noah and his parents having arrived at the venue before them—Noah came straight over to her and took her in his arms.

She stiffened on the instant. But before she could give him a push and demand to know what the blazes he thought he was doing, Noah, obviously feeling the way she tensed up, was grating in her ear, 'Relax! We haven't seen each other for two weeks, remember!'

Oh, that to 'relax' was so easy! His arms were strong, and he was all virile male—bringing to mind what she'd been putting her best efforts into not thinking about—her part in this bargain, and how that must be begun!

Elexa was still at sixes and sevens when, with his back to the rest of the group, Noah pulled back to look into her wide eyes. 'I'm going to have to kiss you,' he said in a low tone.

She roused herself. 'Don't force yourself!' she hissed, offended that it was such an effort for him. But, because her expression was on view, she smiled. His head came down but, because of their watching relatives, it was decorously that he placed his mouth over hers.

Oh, heavens! He had a most superb mouth. She'd had experiments in kissing, but never had she felt that small tingle of electricity that shot through her when she felt the touch of his mouth on hers.

Noah kept an arm about her as he turned with her and apologised for not introducing the two sets of parents straight away. But they smiled indulgently, because naturally, his fiancée would come first with him, and he performed the introductions.

The meal passed off pleasantly, his father and her father getting on famously, with the two mothers seeming to have a great deal in common, too. It appeared Kaye Aston had assumed her daughter would be moving into Noah's home once they were married, and she looked slightly askance when she was informed differently, and the reasons for it. But, as if determined at the outset not to be an interfering mother-in-law, she said nothing.

'Elexa always *was* crazy about her work,' she murmured

instead, going on, 'Most brides-to-be have the day before their wedding off work, I'm sure, but not Elexa. Waldo and I could have taken her home with us tonight, but...'

'We're extremely busy at the office just now,' Elexa inserted. 'And since Lois is staying overnight too, she'll pick me up tomorrow on her way.' Then, feeling a need to change the subject, she turned swiftly to the man she was going to marry. 'Did you manage to arrange your stag night?' she asked, and felt foolish, and wondered where in the Dickens that question had come from—she certainly hadn't given thought to it.

Noah gave her what might have been termed an intimate smile—if you didn't look into the grey depths of his eyes to see that they weren't smiling, intimately or otherwise, but looked more as if to say that he hardly thought it worthwhile to celebrate his last night of freedom, since he had no intention of being bound by marriage for long. But, keeping up the pretence, he answered, 'Marcus said something about coming over.'

A short while later both sets of parents felt that, as they had a bit of a drive, they ought to be on their way. 'You have a lovely daughter, Kaye,' Ruth Peverelle said sincerely as they were leaving.

'And I couldn't ask for a better husband for her than your son,' Kaye Aston replied.

Oh, grief! Elexa refused to study the carpet but, looking up and away from the all but purring mothers, she found she was gazing straight into the eyes of Noah Peverelle— and she was sure from that light in his eyes that he was inwardly laughing.

'We'll take you back to your place first, Elexa,' her mother decided. But just as Elexa was about to acquiesce, Kaye Aston lightly laughed. 'Sorry, Noah. I'm going to have to get out of the habit of being responsible for Elexa's welfare. I was forgetting it's ages since you and Elexa have seen each other. You two will have a lot to talk about, and I'm certain you'll want to be sure Elexa gets home safely.'

For Heaven's sake! She was twenty-five, not fifteen! Elexa didn't want anybody being responsible for her welfare. Though she supposed it was something of a habit her mother had got into.

Elexa stood with Noah and waited as they watched the two sets of parents drive away. 'I'll get a taxi,' she said, coast clear, no need to pretend any more.

'My car's here,' he informed her, and before she could protest that it was no trouble for her to take a taxi, Noah was taking a light hold of her arm and was guiding her to where his car stood.

'I'm sorry to have to put you through all this,' she apologised, once they were seated in his car, realising that he wouldn't give a hoot who knew the true reason why they were marrying.

'It seems a small price to pay to get what I want,' he answered. 'This way you have your peace, in which to concentrate on your job and let your employers know that nobody could do that junior manager's job better than you, and I...'

'Will have your son,' she ended for him—oh, she did so hope she didn't land him with a daughter.

'Exactly,' he agreed, and was pulling up outside her apartment block before she knew it.

Noah got out of the car to walk her to the outside door. She got out her key, and he took it from her, opened the door and handed it back to her. 'I'll see you on Saturday,' he said, by way of parting, and was about to go when Elexa, feeling a touch panicky all of a sudden, halted him.

'We'll have to leave the reception together. In your car. Mine won't be there,' she said in a rush, her words falling over each other.

'It *would* look a bit odd if we departed for our honeymoon in separate directions,' he replied lightly.

But no matter how light his reply, it bothered her. She was used in her work to making everything clear, no room for error. She saw no reason to change that tenet now.

'We're not having a honeymoon!' she told him bluntly.

'I never for a moment thought we were,' he answered equally bluntly, his tone short. She turned away and would have gone quickly through the open door. But suddenly Noah caught a hold of her shoulders and turned her to face him. 'You're strung up about something?' he accused.

'I...' she said about to deny it. But then remembered their conversation about being completely honest with each other. 'I'm uptight, yes,' she admitted. 'I know everything will be all right. It's just th-that—I've never done anything remotely like this before, and—and I suppose there's a part of me that can't believe I'm doing it now.'

Noah Peverelle stared down at her long and hard. 'Do you want to do it?' he questioned—a shade toughly, she rather thought. And to let her know just how desperate he was *not*, added, 'There's time to change your mind if you wish.'

She looked up at him, this slightly arrogant man whom she had approached and more or less asked to marry her. She knew, as her heart gave a little flutter, that once her panic had subsided and she was back to being the logical-thinking female she knew herself to be, she would kick herself if she gave up this chance. This chance of time to herself.

'I've never reneged on a contract in my life,' she answered, and didn't wait to see what he made of that, but went swiftly indoors.

*   *   *

Her wedding day dawned bright and beautiful, and Elexa awoke in her old room in her parents' home feeling very much as she imagined any other bride would. She felt nervous, anxious, and more than a little apprehensive. The only difference being that, while other brides might feel all those emotions, they would also feel excited and look forward to being made 'as one' with the man they were engaged to.

Not that she regretted the decision she had made. Life, barring the occasional problem thrown up in the rush of wedding preparations, had been little short of bliss. Her mother, soon to have her heart's desire and see her daughter 'settled', was at her sweetest. It was so good to be able to answer the telephone and not dread the moment her mother would bring up the subject of some nice man. Such a relief not to pick up the phone to hear how wonderful Jim, Joe or Jeremy was, not to mention Tom, Dick and Harry.

Consequently she and her mother were better friends than they had ever been. If Elexa felt great pangs of guilt every so often that her mother was dewy-eyed about her daughter's marriage, then Elexa realised she would just have to endure that guilt.

Her bedroom door opened and her mother, bearing a breakfast tray, came beaming into the room. 'Here you are, darling! Happy the bride the sun shines on.'

'Mum, you shouldn't have!' Elexa protested as her mother placed the tray over her knees.

'It's a mother's privilege on a day like today.' Kaye Aston gurgled. 'How are you feeling?'

'A bit churned up,' Elexa admitted truthfully.

'You'll be all right when you see Noah,' her mother soothed. 'Now, eat up your breakfast, and don't worry about a thing. Everything's under control. Does Lois eat breakfast these days? She didn't used to.'

The wedding reception was to be held in Elexa's parents' home, and her administrative powers exceptional, Kaye Aston refused to let Elexa 'lift so much as a finger' and left Elexa to go and check lists, cakes and caterers.

The weather held, and at ten minutes to two Elexa looked at her reflection in her bedroom mirror and could not help but know that, in such a beautiful dress, it was impossible not to look good. Though for more than the hundredth time she paused to wonder what she thought she was doing.

It was a bit late in the day to have doubts now. She knew that. There were all her relatives waiting at the church, all Noah's relatives; she would have to go through with it. Not that Noah Peverelle would give a hoot if she didn't show up, but...

Elexa stopped her thoughts right there. She did not know very much about him, this man she was due to marry, this man who was already at the church waiting for her. But what she did know of him, or had gleaned of him, was that he was a proud man. She could not, she realised, not turn up. That would be unforgivable of her.

'Ready, Elexa?' her father coming into the room broke through her last-minute panicky nerves. 'I don't want to get you there early, but your mother would never forgive the rudeness if we arrived late. We should go now, my pet.'

The drive to the church took only a few minutes, but during that time Elexa's feeling of panic took her charging down another avenue. What if Noah had changed *his* mind? What if he wasn't there at the church waiting for her? What if he was the one to decide not to turn up?

They reached the church gates, but there was no Marcus

Dean, Noah's best man, waiting to impart the news that her groom had gone missing. Elexa was still feeling the stress of the situation, however, when, with Joanna and Lois following, she made her way into the church on her father's arm.

The church organ swelled and as they turned to go down the aisle she saw Noah. He had his back to her but stood tall and straight in his morning suit—and proud. Suddenly she wasn't panicking any more. As she and her father walked on, something—she knew not what—seemed to be telling her that to marry Noah was the right thing to do.

Noah turned to glance at her as she reached him. She smiled, and, although he was as sparing as ever with his smiles, he gave her an encouraging look—and the service began.

He did not kiss her after the ceremony, but then tradition had never said that he should. After signing the register they made their way outside, and posed with family and friends for photographs. Then she and Noah were chauffeured back to her old home.

Once there, Elexa stood with Noah in the wide hall ready to greet their guests. It was the first time they had been alone together since the vicar had pronounced them man and wife.

Elexa felt tongue-tied all at once, and turned to Noah, wanting to say something but hardly knowing what it was she wanted to say, only to see that Noah was looking at her, a strangely—dare she believe it?—gentle look in his eyes.

'I—um...' she said nervously, and suddenly he smiled—and her heart fluttered.

'I knew you were beautiful,' Noah, never the flatterer, remarked quietly. 'But today you look absolutely sensational.'

Her heart didn't merely flutter, it thundered. She wanted to say something light—the words, You don't think I'm a bit over-dressed? sprang to her lips. But what she did actually say, was, 'You look a bit dashing yourself,' and, looking at him, saw that she had amused him. Then his parents and her parents arrived, followed in no time by the rest of the guests, and the reception began.

All in all, it was a very pleasant afternoon, with everyone being nice to everyone else. Everyone ate and drank, her father made a speech about letting go his lovely daughter, and Noah made a speech thanking her parents for having such a lovely daughter. Marcus also made a speech— and her mother tried not to notice his three children climbing all over her antique furniture.

Then it was time for Elexa to go up to her room to change into the 'going away' outfit her mother had insisted she purchase, even though everyone knew that, because of Noah's work commitments, they were not going to go away, but would honeymoon later.

Joanna was occupied with baby Betsy, so Lois was delegated to go upstairs with Elexa to help her change. Though, in actual fact, Lois sat on the bed once Elexa was out of her wedding gown, and beamed as she exclaimed, 'What a truly perfect day!'

'I enjoyed it.'

'Were you nervous?'

'Panicking like mad to start with,' Elexa admitted.

'So was I—on my wedding day, I mean. Sorry,' she immediately apologised, 'shouldn't have brought that up— mine ended in divorce.'

Strangely, when she knew full well that her marriage was scheduled to end in divorce too, Elexa experienced the oddest pang—almost as if she did not want it to.

'Do I look all right?' she asked quickly, smoothing down the jacket of her new blue suit.

'How does fantastic sound?' Almost as good as sensational, Elexa thought; wasn't that what Noah had said, that she looked absolutely sensational? 'You've gone all dreamy-eyed,' Lois teased. 'Come on, let me get you back to your man.'

Noah had changed out of morning dress into a well-cut suit he'd had in his car. 'Shall we say our goodbyes to the parents?' he suggested, which took about a half-hour, because there were aunts, uncles and others who wished to be included.

They left the house to cheers and well-wishes, but Elexa almost dropped when she saw what had been done to Noah's Jaguar—balloons, streamers, tin cans, everything but the kitchen sink had been attached to it.

'I can't ride in that!' she gasped, seeing her cousin Rory's hand in all this.

'You won't have to,' said the man who thought of everything, and holding up a car key, he announced, 'I've swapped cars with Marcus.' She laughed—she quite liked this husband of hers.

On the way back to London, however, she decided not to think of him as her husband. To do so might make him a permanent fixture in her life, and he was anything but that.

Once they drew up outside her flat, it seemed not quite the done thing just to say a brief goodbye and leave him— her wedding ring was still new on her finger. But, then again, there didn't seem to be any point in inviting him up for a coffee or something. Married they might be, but they didn't have that sort of a relationship.

She searched for something in between. 'Thank you for today,' she said, thinking that just about covered it. Then all at once she realised that Noah had that day completed his part of their bargain, but that still left her side of the bargain to be completed. 'Er—I'll—er work something out and be in touch,' she murmured, turning her suddenly-burning face away from him as she sought the car door handle.

'I'll wait to hear from you,' Noah answered easily—and she was still fumbling with the door handle when he came round and opened it for her.

She stepped out onto the pavement, diving into her bag for her door key. He opened that door for her too, handing her back the key. She looked at him. Not too many hours ago she had married him; *he* was her husband. 'Er—goodbye,' she mumbled.

He looked down at her and she knew he was aware of her feeling of awkwardness when, for a moment, she thought she saw a hint of devilment in his eyes before, bending, he placed his warm mouth against her cheek and kissed her. 'Goodbye,' he said, then added, 'er—dear,' and as they drew apart they both burst out laughing.

It was a wonderful moment. A kind of treasured moment of mutual laughter that totally eased away her feeling of awkwardness. Then she became aware that Noah was no longer laughing but was staring down at her solemn-eyed. An instant later he had turned from her and was striding back to his car.

She did not want to still be there, should he glance over to her when he got to the driver's door. Abruptly she went in and quickly closed the door behind her. She ignored the stairs for once and went to the lift. It had been quite a day.

For the first time ever, Elexa found Sunday unbearable. So far as anyone knew, she and Noah would not wish to be disturbed—wherever they were. Consequently her telephone stayed silent. Not that, under the circumstances, she would have answered it had it rung. By the same token, she was unable to telephone anyone for a chat.

That in itself did not bother her unduly. It was just that she had started to feel very unsettled—restless, somehow. She took herself off for a walk, but still felt as unsettled and restless when she returned.

She supposed the fact that yesterday had been so eventful could have something to do with it. Many were the times she thought of Noah. Was he having a not-answering-the-phone-day too? Another thought struck—and she didn't like it—was he perhaps on the phone at this very minute talking to one of his lady-friends? She hardly expected him to give them up. Perhaps he was out with one of them right at this very moment. Without another thought Elexa snatched her wedding ring from her finger.

She was glad to see Monday. Glad to be going to work. She had last week told Des Reynolds when he came on the prowl that she was going out with someone, but, because she didn't want any fuss at the office, she'd thought she would leave telling anyone there that she was going to be married until it was *fait accompli.*

'You've forsaken me for another!' Des had gasped, clutching his heart.

'Clear off—and bother somebody else.'

With Jamie Hodges, when he had come into her office with that light in his eyes that hinted he was about to ask her out, she had been a little more diplomatic. 'Jamie, I've met someone,' she'd told him quietly, and had gone on to tell him that she was going steady.

He'd argued that it was quick, that she hadn't said anything about it the last time he'd asked her out. 'Why didn't you say something then?'

'How could I? I didn't know if anything would come of it at the time.'

Elexa drove to the offices of Colman and Fisher having decided not to wear her wedding ring or her engagement ring. Her wedding was too recent still. Perhaps as a passing kind of comment she would mention some time—if she remembered, she thought sniffily—that she had married.

Idris Young, one of her team, stopped by her office that Monday to invite her to a party he and his wife were having on Saturday. She enjoyed parties, but somehow didn't feel in a partying mood. Absurdly she suddenly thought of Noah, of Noah partying—he worked hard; he probably played with equal vigour.

'I'd love to come,' she accepted Idris's invite cheerfully.

Annoyingly, when she had always before found her job completely absorbing, thoughts of Noah Peverelle seemed to constantly come between her and her work. She supposed it must be quite natural. For goodness' sake, she was married to him! Only last Saturday she had married him. Grief, she hadn't been married to him for a week yet!

Elexa went home in a solemn frame of mind. Hers was not a proper marriage. But, she reminded herself, Noah had married her, and in doing so had completed his part of the bargain they had made. He was now waiting to hear from her so she should begin to complete her part.

Relieved that she had a computer at home, and that she wasn't at risk of anyone coming in and spotting what she was doing, Elexa switched on her computer as soon as she got in. She owned that, though intelligent enough to cope easily with her very stressful job, she was totally at sea when it came to knowing when her fertile period was— she hadn't a clue how to work it out. If they'd taught it at school she must have either been away that day, or had her head filled with other matter.

The Internet gave her the answer. At least, she thought it did. She printed off various pieces of information, read everything through several times, and got on with calculations. By the time she had worked out what she was fairly certain must be the right dates, Elexa was all churned up inside. It would seem that she would be in a position to contact Noah next week.

Elexa full well knew that she could have phoned him at any time to tell him of her findings, but the rest of the week went by without her once dialling his number. She wasn't trying to get out of it, she told herself. It was purely that it seemed to her to call for a little more delicacy than just to ring him with the bold request that he leave next Wednesday evening free.

By Saturday night, the night of Idris Young's party, Elexa had still not telephoned Noah. 'Enjoying yourself?' Paul—that was what she thought his name was—asked.

'Super,' she replied, and listened with half an ear as he chatted away, until it became obvious he was leading up to asking her out. 'I'm spoken for,' she interrupted him.

'Where is he?' Paul asked looking around. 'I wouldn't neglect you if…'

'I'm sure you wouldn't,' she smiled, and, since she'd accepted the invitation, made a great effort to be a good guest, and went through the motions of asking him what sort of work he did, and appeared to listen intently until a moment came when she could make her escape.

She arrived home around midnight, the party long gone from her mind. She went to her bedroom and, slipping her shoes off, spotted her wedding ring where she had left it on her dressing table. For no reason, she slipped it on. Noah Peverelle, and how she must give him a call, again occupied her mind, much as it had all that week.

But, in the act of unzipping her dress, she stopped, startled, when her phone suddenly rang. She looked at her watch: ten past twelve! Who on earth— The sound of the telephone ringing had been remarkable by its absence that week. Fearing some emergency, she hurried to answer it.

'Hello?' she enquired urgently.

'Where the hell have you been?' snarled an aggressive harsh male voice.

Noah? He sounded more annoyed than worried, so Elexa realised that nobody had fallen down and broken a leg. 'I've been to a party,' she replied, as evenly as she could in the circumstances.

'Who with?' he gritted bossily.

She'd had enough of him! Nobody bossed her around. 'You sound like some irate husband,' she answered acidly.

'That's because I *am* a husband. Yours! If you're playing around—' He broke off, but only for a moment, because in the next instant he was snarling, 'When you have that baby, I want to know for certain that it's mine!'

If he was furious, she was outraged. 'You *pig!*' she yelled, and slammed the phone down on him.

Tears spurted to her eyes. How could he? How *could* he? The phone rang again; she ignored it. It carried on ringing—she went into the bathroom and drowned out the sound by taking a shower.

She was still outraged when, nightdress-and-dressing-gown-clad, she paced about her sitting-room. Then the door buzzer sounded. She stopped pacing and automatically glanced at her wrist. She wasn't wearing a watch, but knew, if it wasn't Saturday-night revellers going along ringing doorbells for a lark, that it would have taken Noah Peverelle half an hour to get here.

She went to the intercom. 'Yes!' she snapped.

'I don't find apologising very easy.'

'Don't strain yourself!'

'I think I should do it face to face.'

'I'll get the sackcloth and ashes ready!' she hissed, but thumped the button to let him up.

He wasn't long in getting there. She had left the door ajar and he came straight in, quietly closing the door behind him. 'I rang earlier—to let you know I was back.'

'I didn't know you'd been away!'

'You're determined to give me a hard time.'

'Nobody talks to me like that!' she flared. *'Nobody!'* She wanted to hate him, but found that she didn't.

'I was out of order. I can't tell you how sorry I am.'

'You still don't trust me.'

'That's the hell of it,' he answered. 'I rather think I do.'

'Rather?'

'Okay, then, yes, I do. I suppose, after chasing around this week sorting out various crises, for some unknown reason I imagined you enjoying a phone-free week staying home in your apartment.' He had thought about her—as she had thought about him? It weakened her anger— briefly. No doubt he'd only thought of her in the context of when the Dickens she was going to contact him. 'I never gave thought that you might be living it up somewhere. It—annoyed me that I'd made several phone calls to you this evening and that it was gone midnight before you came home.'

Elexa studied the tall, grey-eyed, stern-faced man in front of her. They had spoken of honesty with each other and, in his apology, he couldn't have been more honest. 'The party was just getting going when I left.'

'You weren't enjoying it?'

She smiled. Against her will, she smiled. 'Does that please you?'

'Why should you have all the fun?'

'While you slave? Er...' She hesitated. 'Do I take it that you haven't partied recently?'

Noah gave her a steady look. 'If you're asking have I taken anybody out since we married, then the answer is that I haven't. Nor do I intend to while we are married.'

Elexa stared at him for a moment or two, and then found she was asking, 'Er—can I get you a coffee?'

'Am I forgiven for my swinish remark?'

She looked into his sincere grey eyes. He had said he trusted her. What was to forgive? He wouldn't have said that he trusted her if he didn't mean it. 'Of course,' she replied.

He half smiled then, though his smile didn't fully make it. 'Then I'll go,' he said. He was halfway to the door when he abruptly turned back, and, scrutinising her face, 'You know, of course, that you're just as beautiful without make-up.'

Her hand went straight to her scrubbed cheek. 'My stars, Mr Peverelle,' she managed, 'when you apologise you certainly do it in style.' His lips twitched, and this time he did smile. It gave her the spurt of courage she needed to tell him what she had to tell him. Albeit that he had reached the hall door of her apartment before she cried, 'Noah!'—a touch croakily, it had to be admitted.

He turned, his attention all hers. 'Elexa?' he queried, perhaps picking up that note of tension.

'I—er... I—um... I've been—er checking...' she blurted out in a sudden rush, feeling red right down to her toes but forcing herself on. 'And...and...and Wednesday night seems—er—favourable.' If he asked 'favourable for what?' she was going to die on the spot.

He didn't ask, but was as quick on the uptake as she knew him to be. But, when she was just about drowning with embarrassment, he asked coolly, 'Would you like to come over to my place, or would you prefer I came here?' calmly giving her the choice of venue.

She hadn't got that far in her thinking, but quickly realised that, once it was over, she would probably want to be by herself. 'I'll come over to you,' she opted. That way she could say thank you very much, or whatever it was that one said on those occasions, and get out of there.

'Come and have some dinner with me,' he invited.

'I'm working late on Wednesday,' she invented rapidly. 'I'll have a sandwich sent in, and get to your place as soon as I can.'

His steady grey eyes stayed on her face. 'Till then,' he said—and left her desperately trying to get herself back together again. If she was feeling shaky now, what in creation was she going to be like on Wednesday?

CHAPTER FIVE

By Monday Elexa was close to being a nervous wreck. She didn't want to go through with it, she knew that she didn't. Had anyone offered her an alternative, she would have grabbed at it. But nobody did. There was no alternative.

Again and again during sleepless hours she had made herself remember that Noah trusted her. He had completed his side of the bargain, and he'd trusted her to go to him and begin to fulfil her side. It was of no help to her, however, to also remember the strength of Noah's firm arms around her that night at the Falcon Restaurant. She remembered, too, the feel of his warm mouth against her own in that decorous, chaste kiss. Oh, Lord, the time for chaste kisses was over!

Elexa was pleased to get into work, to be able to fix her thoughts elsewhere. 'Terrific party, Idris,' she complimented him warmly when she stopped by his desk.

'Paul said you were serious about someone. You should have brought him.'

'He works away a lot,' she answered, and went to her own office wondering, had Noah been home by then, would he have accepted to go to the party with her?

Suddenly she realised the way she was thinking. For Heaven's sake, she and Noah didn't have that sort of relationship. They were married, yes, but in a platonic, not even friends, kind of way. Platonic? Oh, crikey!

By Wednesday, having thrown herself into her work in the hope of forgetting that pay-back time was at hand,

Elexa had achieved all that she could achieve. At seven o'clock that evening, with all other offices she might have wanted to contact now long since closed, there was little more she could do.

She looked at her watch, at what she was sure was an hour later, only to see that it was not yet seven-fifteen. Feeling extremely fidgety, she cleared her desk and went to the car park.

She wasn't using delaying tactics, she convinced herself as she started up her vehicle, but she did not want to get there too early and find Noah in the middle of eating his dinner. She drove to her flat and, the hours seeming to have stood still, leaving her with ample time to spare, she took a shower. With her nerves starting to fray, she suddenly wanted it over and done with.

She was about to leave her apartment when it dawned on her that she didn't know how these things went. What she suddenly did know though, was that there was no way she could get into his bed without a stitch on.

Elexa went hot and then cold at the thought and speedily emptied out her briefcase, collected a fresh nightdress from a drawer, added her toothbrush and paste, and hurriedly departed her flat before her feet became cemented to the floor.

She drove on autopilot, trying to keep her mind a blank—an impossibility, she discovered. And all at once—unfairly, she owned, even as her thoughts raced—she started to blame Noah Peverelle because she felt as jumpy as a kitten. Had he consented to scientific means rather than natural she wouldn't be in this almighty stew.

Perhaps she would feel better once she was there, once she saw him.

She did not feel better. It was almost nine when he answered the door to her ring. Noah, looking as stern as mostly always, invited her in. 'Do you normally work this late?' he enquired levelly, indicating her briefcase. Then, to her relief, he ignored the stairs and took her into his drawing-room.

'I w-went home,' she stammered. 'I—um—needed to freshen up.' Oh grief, that was wrong; she didn't want him thinking she had showered for his benefit. 'I—er—one gets grubby at work,' she added. 'You know how it is,' she rattled on, her all-on-edge feelings making her tongue gallop away.

Noah stared at her. 'Have a seat,' he suggested quietly, his eyes never leaving her face—she would have given anything to know what he was thinking. 'What can I get you to drink?' he offered.

She didn't want a drink. Neither did she want to sit down. What she wanted was this over with all speed so she could race home to her own bed. 'N-nothing,' she answered. 'Thank you,' she added belatedly, jerkily.

Standing about a yard away, he studied her still standing form. 'You sound on edge,' he observed, in that same quiet tone.

Well, top marks for spotting that! He annoyed her. 'It's not every day I—I—er—with someone I barely know,' she retorted—and soon found that he cared not for her tone.

'I'm your husband!' he rapped.

'I've never had one of those before either!' she flared unthinkingly, wanting to be pleasant, but nerves, his tone, causing her to fire back.

She saw his brow shoot up. 'You're a—' He broke off, but was already discounting the notion, and did not utter the word. But he was in demanding frame of mind, she soon realised, when he abruptly challenged, 'Just how many partners have you had?'

Her face flamed; she knew she must be scarlet. But she

refused to be intimidated by anybody, and that included him. 'If you behave yourself—I'll have a count of one!'

Oh, he didn't like that, did he? Though which part, she was unsure. 'Are you saying that you never have before?' he was back to demanding harshly.

'I've been busy!' she snapped.

'Hell's teeth—you're a virgin!' He didn't look best pleased.

'It's not a crime!'

'You misled me!' he accused harshly. She knew that she had, and had no defence. She had let him think that she hadn't had many partners, which she knew he had interpreted as her having had some. 'You deliberately let me believe...'

She'd had enough of him. She didn't want to be here anyway. 'Oh, shut up,' she cut him off—and saw his expression go from angry to one of being totally fed up.

'Oh, go to bed!' he gritted shortly, obviously unable to bear the sight of her.

Who on earth did he think he was? she fumed, stung. 'Like blazes, I'll go to bed!' she erupted. Who did he think he was that he could tell her pithily where to go! And imagine she would go! He knew what he could do with his dishonourable intentions! 'I'm going home!' she informed him spiritedly, and didn't wait to hear what he made of that, but went storming out from the room and down the long hall.

By the time she reached his front door, however, her fury with him had subsided a little. Sufficiently, anyhow, for her to realise that if anybody was acting dishonourably here, it was her. She stretched out a hand to the doorknob, but when she went to turn it—she found that she could not. Physically she could, but—but honourably, she could not.

Elexa stayed like that for some seconds with her hand on the doorknob. Then slowly, defeated, she let her hand fall to her side. She turned about, as in all honesty she knew that she must. But when she looked back along the hall she saw that Noah had come out from the drawing-room and had been watching her.

She swallowed hard. She was the one who had started this. She was the one who had made that initial phone call. Slowly she began to walk back towards him. She paused for a second on the way to place her briefcase down upon the stairs that led to the upstairs rooms. Straightening, she looked to where Noah, his eyes on her every move, was still standing, and carried on walking towards him.

She was but a step away when she halted. 'I'm sorry,' she mumbled, realising that he must be wanting all this over as quickly as she did.

Elexa was staring at a button on his shirt when he said quietly, 'No—I apologise,' and, when her head jerked up, 'You're scared stiff—and I don't like being the one forced to wear the black hat.'

That surprised her. Surprised her that he was admitting to such sensitivity, surprised her that he didn't like being forced to be the baddy. It made him less of the stern person she knew him to be. It made him warmer, somehow.

'Sh-shall I go—er—up?' she began. 'I don't know which room. Um…'

For a second or two he just stood studying her face. Then, taking a step to her side, 'I'll come with you,' he said.

'Fine,' she answered, somehow managing to sound far calmer than she felt.

With a guiding hand beneath her elbow, Noah steered her to the stairs, but let go to collect her briefcase. Together they ascended the stairs, but once he had shown her into his bedroom he went back to the door. Now, she realised, was not the time to panic.

'I've a few phone calls to make,' he excused himself, and left her.

At first her eyes focussed on nothing. Instinctively she seemed to know that the phone calls he had to make were non-existent. He was just giving her some minute's respite, perhaps to change and get in to bed, perhaps to calm down a little.

Picking up her briefcase, she took it into the adjoining bathroom and washed her face, cleaned her teeth and rapidly got changed. She did not want to be caught standing around in her cotton nightdress when he returned, so went from the bathroom to observe the dark mahogany of the bedroom furniture, the masculine look of the room.

She went over to the double bed but had no idea on which side he slept. Though she realised her feeling of tension must have scrambled her brain and that he probably didn't have a 'side' but more probably slept in the middle.

Elexa went to climb into the side nearest to her, then realised the central light was on. There were switches on the wall by the bed head. She experimented. Out went the main light, on came a wall-light.

She got into bed and switched off the light shining above her. The darkness and the strange room combined to make her feel more jumpy than ever. With her breath catching in her throat, she turned the wall-light on again, then heard faint sounds that told her she was about to have company.

Hurriedly she turned her back to the door—which meant she was facing the middle of the bed. Swiftly she shunted over to the other side—just as the door opened.

The door closed, then she heard the bathroom door open

and close and, her ears sharp for every sound, she heard Noah taking a shower. Instinct made her want to pretend to be asleep. But that wasn't in the contract. Noah was an honourable man—he deserved the same from her.

Nevertheless, she tensed rigid when she heard the bathroom door open. She wanted to be nice about this, wanted to be pleasant. Oh, please help her not to let the side down.

Elexa was striving with all she had to relax when she felt Noah get into bed beside her. She was grateful to him that, as if appreciating she had left the light on until she was accustomed to her surroundings, he too left it on.

But everything tightened up within her when Noah said softly, 'Come here,' and, not waiting for her to comply, reached for her. She felt his hands on her shoulders and, when he manoeuvred her into his arms, she strove hard to be compliant.

Her bare arm touched his naked chest, and her skin felt scorched. She had an idea that the bed cover was all he wore—but she wasn't much into the business of wanting to find out for sure.

She started to tremble, but, strangely, as Noah moved her head on to his shoulder and she willed herself to co-operate, she discovered that there was nothing to co-operate with—because instead of starting to make love to her, Noah seemed more interested in having—*a chat*!

'What sort of a week did you have last week?' he asked conversationally.

'Er—average,' she sort of mumbled.

'No telephone calls?'

'The phone's always frantic. Oh!' She cottoned on. He meant calls from her mother. 'You mean at home? It's been bliss, pure and simple,' she told him, and even found she was smiling. 'What sort of week did you have?'

'Wherever possible I conduct meetings over a video

link,' he replied. 'When that isn't possible, or when I want to take a look around, I take a plane.'

'Like last week?'

'I spent last week mainly visiting some of our overseas people,' he confirmed, and for some minutes spoke quietly about some of the business he had conducted. Elexa very slowly began to fractionally relax.

Her trembling began to ease, but she was still very aware of him next to her. Aware of the firm shoulder her head was resting on. Aware of his skin against her neck. Aware of the clean smell of him. And more aware of him than ever when his other arm came across her and he began stroking her bare arm.

Nervously she looked up at him, her eyes searching his. He smiled encouragingly. 'Are you going to throw a fit if I kiss you?' he asked lightly.

Her heart thumped. 'I wish you would,' she replied huskily.

His hand left her arm and gently he trailed the backs of his fingers down the side of her face. 'I know you want this over with all speed—' he let her know he was alive to how she was feeling '—but this way will be better for you, believe me.' She stared up at him, her lovely brown eyes large and innocent. 'Trust me,' he said softly.

She wanted to tell him that trust him she did, but her throat seemed locked suddenly of further words. Then he was adjusting his position, and his head was coming down, blocking out the light.

'It will be all right,' Noah murmured softly, and Elexa felt the thistledown kiss of his lips against her own.

He pulled back, his eyes studying her face. She rather guessed he was looking to see how his kiss had been received. Suddenly she was liking him more than she had ever liked him that, when he could have quickly, perhaps roughly, taken her, the sooner to get it over with, he was making love to her at a pace that catered for her untried state.

She smiled up at him. This was a mutual bargain here, and all at once she wanted to help all she could. 'That was—nice,' she whispered shyly, and was rewarded with a smile.

Keeping one arm around her shoulders, Noah again kissed her, then gently kissed her again, his free hand stroking in tender movements over her shoulder and down her arm.

Elexa wanted to co-operate and placed a nervous arm over his shoulders, the feel of his naked skin little short of electrifying to her. Then bravely she reached up and placed her lips against his in a giving kiss.

When Noah next kissed her, there was a hint of the passion to come in his kiss. Yet it was still gently that he parted her lips with his own. Elexa felt hot all over, and Noah pulled back to look into her flushed face. 'Try not to be afraid,' he instructed quietly.

She smiled—she had never dreamed he would be so gentle, so caring in his lovemaking. 'I don't think I am— so much,' she answered, and felt all sort of funny inside when, after giving her one of his gently scrutinising looks, he kissed her again, something flickering into life inside her when she felt the tip of his tongue against lips.

Again he moved her, but this time so that she was lying with her back flat against the mattress. When his body came halfway over her, she clutched on to him hard. Again he kissed her and, of its own volition, her other arm seemed to come up and around him, and she found she was experimenting herself, the tip of her tongue touching his mouth.

'You—um—taste—n-nice,' she said, and was held more

tightly to him for a moment. Then great alarm bells were going off in her head when Noah began to caress her body, and his hand caressed closer, ever closer to her breast. Instinctively she knocked his hand away when it came too close—but she was instantly apologetic. 'I'm sorry, I'm sorry,' she cried quickly, apologetically.

'Shh…' he quieted her soothingly.

She wanted to make amends, badly wanted to make amends. 'I'm ashamed of myself. Sh-shall I take my night-dress off?' she offered.

'My word, you really are sorry,' he teased, and she found she liked his teasing. When next his caressing hand and fingers neared her breast she did not flinch. 'You're allowed to breathe,' Noah murmured against her ear, aware that she seemed to be holding her breath. She exhaled on a sigh of sound when his right hand sought and captured her left breast.

A fire started to ignite in her at his touch. 'Oh,' she cried in a little thrill of sound when his gentle fingers caressed the hardened nub.

'Oh, yes? Or oh, no?' he questioned softly.

'You know,' she answered, and she was sure he did.

'Shall we try without this?' he asked, tweaking the cotton of her nightdress.

He would have helped her, but she discovered, fire or no fire, that she wasn't yet ready to totally do away with years of modesty. 'I'll do it,' she insisted, and held the duvet close to her form while she wriggled out of her only garment.

She was still clutching the bed cover to her when she lay down again. Noah leaned over and kissed her and, his arm coming under the duvet, he placed his other arm around her. She felt his caress to her naked skin and could not help but tense up. Noah stilled for a few seconds, but the next time he kissed her there was a hint of more passion there, and as her insides became a nonsense, Elexa could do no other than put her arms around him, drawing him closer.

He came farther under the duvet to her and she felt his hair-roughened chest against her naked breasts. She kissed him, giving herself up to his kisses as gently, tenderly he caressed her breasts, making yet more of a nonsense of her when he bent down further and kissed the swollen globes, taking the tip of one breast into his mouth.

'Noah!' she cried in pleasure, her body moving involuntarily.

He raised his head and looked into her eyes. What he saw there she had no idea, but suddenly he moved briefly from her, and the next she knew he had plunged the room into darkness.

When he came back to her she hungrily sought his mouth. She wanted to cry his name again, but instead heard him groan hers. 'Elexa,' he murmured, his voice kind of hoarse. Then he was kissing her with a passion she had never dreamed of, and she wanted him.

Or thought she did. But that was until his hands caressed down her body to her behind, and gently he began to draw her to him. Her heart seemed to miss several beats, and the next she knew was that, as if wanting, needing, to feel her silken body against him, he had drawn her fully up against his hard, wanting, all-male body—and on that instant shock hit her, making her gasp.

Jerkily, abruptly, without having to think about it, just acting on what she knew to be right, what she knew to be wrong, Elexa pushed him violently away. 'No!' she cried, scrabbling to sit up, taking the bed cover with her. Panicking wildly, she sat there—blinking as Noah moved at speed to switch on the light. He was sitting up too, his broad expanse of chest causing her to swallow. Never had she been so intimate with any man. 'I can't do this!' she gasped, and knew that he would be furious with her and that the least he would do would be to throw her out. Nor would she blame him.

Wild-eyed, clutching the duvet to her as Noah stared stern-faced at her, she strove miserably to get herself together. Then, even as she waited for a tongue-lashing, suddenly, as she warily watched him, to her utter amazement Noah started to smile the most wonderful smile—and at that moment her heart went crazy. And as he commented, 'It's a bit late to start a game of Monopoly, but if you fancy a cup of tea I'll go and make you one,' then laughed a quite wonderful laugh, so her panic fled—and she fell in love with him.

'Oh, Noah,' she wailed, and to make love with this man suddenly didn't seem alien any more. To make love with this man whom she had just realised held her heart seemed all at once only right. 'Are you going to forgive me my moment of panic—and let me try again?' she asked tremulously.

His serious expression was back, but it didn't matter. She had seen him smile when she had thought the least he would do would be to strangle her. She had heard him laugh when all the odds had been against him doing anything of the sort. She loved him!

'You're sure, Elexa?'

'I'm sure,' she answered, and dropped her modest hold on the duvet she held in front of her. 'I'm sure,' she repeated, and stayed sure when his glance went from her face down to her firm, pink-tipped, swollen breasts.

'You're beautiful,' he murmured.

I'm yours, she wanted to tell him. I'm your wife. But, because she couldn't tell him, she showed him that she was his by raising her arms and placing her forearms on his shoulders.

'Elexa, my dear,' he breathed, his hands coming to her waist. Gently he touched his mouth to hers and, when she responded, she felt his hands caress from her waist to the sides of her breasts, causing her more breathlessness when he captured each hard-tipped globe in his hands.

She could not hold in the moan of wanting when she felt the smooth caress of his touch as he tenderly moulded her breasts. She luxuriated in the feel of his fingers, his mouth, when he bent to give and take pleasure as he kissed her breasts, his tongue caressing the stiff peak he had created.

She almost cried out that she loved him, but she couldn't tell him that either. So instead, as he raised his head to look deeply into her eyes, she shyly suggested, 'Do we need this light on?'

He paused, but only for a moment. Then the room was in darkness once more. Tenderly he continued to stroke and caress her body, taking her to new unimagined heights. Still kissing her, he at last brought her to lie down with him—his mouth on hers with a gentle, yet more passionate intensity—and Elexa gloried in their closeness.

Again and again he kissed her, and again and again she returned his kisses. There was no need to hold back any longer. She loved him—what could be more right?

Her senses were soaring when, wanting to get closer, yet closer to him, Elexa let go more of her inhibitions and moved so that the whole length of her body was against his. She pressed against him, and heard his groan of wanting, and for long wonderful moments he held her to him. Then gently he rolled her onto her back, and kissed her, trailing kisses down over her face and throat.

His mouth was against her mouth again when his caressing touch moved down, lingering over her breasts, and whispered down to the softness of her belly. She moaned his name in her need. 'Noah, Noah,' she cried, and from her inexperience, 'I want you—but I don't know what to do.'

'Do what feels right to you, my dear,' he murmured, and as he kissed her his caressing hands thrilled her with each intimately investigating touch as his fingers roved over her hips, and more intimately still, causing her to catch her breath.

'Noah!' she whispered on an indrawn gasp of jerky sound.

'Please don't tell me *now* that you can't,' he urged.

'Oh, I can,' she replied huskily, 'I can,' and was aware that, when soon she would welcome him, only she would know that it was with so much love in her heart.

CHAPTER SIX

FOR many hours that night Elexa lay sleepless in bed beside Noah. Many thoughts drifted through her mind, but never once did she recall her intention that as soon as she had conceived Noah's child she was going to race out of his home and back to her flat with all speed.

Oh, she loved him so. Was this why it had seemed so right to marry him? Was this the reason why she had been so restless of late? Wasn't it odd how you speculated on love, what it was, and how did you know when you were in love? But when you knew—it was just—there. She had never expected to find love, nor had she particularly wanted to. But it had just…happened. Arrived. Was there. It was just there, and you knew it, couldn't not recognise it.

Oh, hadn't he been wonderful? She remembered his lovemaking, his kisses, and her heart swelled fit to burst. She wanted to stretch out, to touch him. But that, to fall in love with him, had not been a part of the bargain.

Dreamily she thought of those intimate moments with him. He had been, oh so gentle with her, tender, sensitive. Knowing he would have to hurt her, he had held back, tempered his passion to try and make it less painful for her.

'Shh,' he had steadied her at one time when, in her love for him, she had wanted to give him pleasure and had moved too eagerly, only for a small cry of pain to take her. Noah had stilled, had held her quiet until her pain had gone. Then, gently kissing her, he had aroused her again and all pain had been forgotten.

She glanced at the illuminated bedside clock and saw that it was four-thirty. She knew that she should get up and leave, but she did not want to. She would never lie with Noah again, be this close with him, and she wanted to savour every second.

Elexa was still wide awake a half an hour later when Noah moved and got out of bed. He did not put on the light, but even so she quickly closed her eyes, shyness overcoming her. Shyness, and a sudden uncertainty that Noah might well be surprised to have woken up to find her still there. Perhaps he expected her to have left by now.

But, no, as she heard him moving around, heard the bathroom door open then close, she discounted that thought, recalling how Noah had remained gentle and tender. How afterwards he had sensitively kissed her and brushed the cloud of hair back from her face.

'Is everything all right with you?' he had asked softly.

'Y-yes,' she'd whispered back.

'You feel—comfortable? Do you need anything?'

He had been so solicitous of her newly awakened and perhaps tender body, that, her heart full, she had again wanted to tell him that she loved him. 'Nothing,' she'd answered, whispering in the darkness. 'It was—I didn't know quite what to expect.'

'You don't regret it?'

She had wanted to tell him how much she did not regret it, how much she, in her love for him, wanted to hold nothing back. 'I'm glad I'm not a virgin any more,' she had said shyly.

And when there had been no need, he had kissed her tenderly again, and urged, 'Get some rest now,' and, trailing gentle fingers down her face, 'Go to sleep, Elexa,' he'd instructed, and then moved from her as if to assure himself that she would rest, would sleep more easily if there was space between them. When, in actual fact, what she had wanted to do was to rest, to sleep in the harbour of his arms.

She heard the shower running and guessed that Noah had an early start, needed to be somewhere. Perhaps he had a plane to catch or perhaps he was driving somewhere for an eight o'clock meeting.

She had opened her eyes, but closed them the moment she heard the bathroom door open again. She kept them closed while drawers whispered open, while a wardrobe was quietly opened. In fact, in the grip of an overwhelming shyness, she kept her eyes closed until she heard the bedroom door open and shut, and knew that she was alone.

The moment Noah had left, she regretted that she hadn't said hello, or something. Anything to have some sort of communication with him. Should she get up, go downstairs, say good morning? Shyness once more swamped her, and kept her riveted to the bed.

She jumped when someone rang the doorbell. Then she heard various sounds and realised that a company driver must have come to pick Noah up. Then all was silent and it was too late. Already she wanted to see him again. Perhaps he had left her a note? Get real, why would he? What would he say?

Noah had not left her a note, Elexa found when, showered and dressed by six o'clock, she'd gone downstairs. Even knowing that there was no earthly reason why he should leave her a note, she could not help but take a look in the drawing-room and in the kitchen before she left.

Disappointed, and all too soon realising that to be so much in love with someone was an extremely anxious business, Elexa drove to her home to change and go about her own business.

She later drove to her office, knowing that she must never forget that Noah's lovemaking with her had been purely a means to an end. He did not love her, nor ever would—he was much too busy for such nonsense—so she had better establish that in her head at the start. He hadn't asked for her love, and definitely did not want it.

Elexa pulled up at the offices of Colman and Fisher, having accepted that sad truth. But, love ever hopeful, she wanted to believe that, when this was all over, the divorce done with, she and Noah might finish up as friends.

She had been at her desk a couple of hours when, for the umpteenth time that morning, her phone rang. She picked it up and was advised by Faith, the company telephonist, that there was a call for her from Germany.

Germany! So far as Elexa knew she wasn't dealing with any client from Germany—but there was always a first time. 'Hello?' she enquired pleasantly, and nearly dropped when she heard the voice of the man she had lain with only a few long hours ago.

'Noah,' he announced. And as her heart did cartwheels, he continued, 'I just wanted to know that you made it to work without any problem.'

Oh, Noah, Noah, how kind, my darling, 'Y-yes. No—um—problem.'

'I've caught you at a bad moment?'

'No. No,' she quickly assured him, terrified he would go and this wonderful moment would be too soon over.

'And...' He paused. 'You're all right? You feel okay?'

On top of the lovely, lovely world. 'I feel fine,' she toned it down.

'Good,' he said, and it sounded as if he was smiling. 'I'll get on with some work, then.'

'Goodbye,' she said, and put down the phone wondering if being in love had made her senseless or what? Had she not said goodbye, he might have stayed talking a little longer. Love, she was discovering, had neither pride nor sense. But wasn't it lovely of Noah, when he was always so up to his eyes in work, to have taken time out of his busy day to find out if her introduction to lovemaking had left her with trauma of any description?

'You've gone all dreamy-looking,' Carol, one of her team, appeared at her elbow.

Elexa came to, realising she still had her hand on the phone. 'That was my husband,' she answered, before she'd got her head back together, and only realised what she had just said when Carol let out a scream of astonishment and delight.

'You're *married*!' she yelled, and as Idris Jones followed her into Elexa's office Carol turned to him, 'Did you know Elexa got married?' she asked.

An hour later and Elexa felt as if there wasn't an employee in the large concern of Colman and Fisher who didn't know that, not only did she have a husband, but also knew who he was, what he did, and the fact that he was out of the country working at the moment.

By five that evening, nothing would do but for them to take her to their usual watering hole to celebrate. Elexa, who had been in on some of these sessions herself—one had gone on way past midnight—would by far have preferred to have gone home. From memory she hadn't had any sleep at all last night, and her bed was calling.

She eventually managed to arrive home at nine o'clock, let herself in to hear her telephone ringing, and fairly flew to answer it. 'Hello,' she gasped, only for her heart to settle to a dull beat. It was not Noah—though why she should suppose he should ring twice in one day she couldn't think. Love, she realised, had made her irrational.

'I tried to get you last night, but you weren't there,' her mother stated.

'I—we,' Elexa corrected, remembering as far as her family was concerned she was a 'we' now. 'We were at Noah's.'

'And tonight you're at your place?'

'Noah's in Germany,' Elexa replied, realising that since it wasn't such a long flight he might in all probability be back in England again.

'Oh, poor you,' Kaye Aston sympathised. 'Never mind, darling, he'll soon be home again. I would have rung before, but for all you didn't go away I considered you to be on your honeymoon. Even so, Noah won't want me clogging up your phone every five minutes. The reason I rang,' she began to explain, although from memory Elexa could never remember her mother needing a reason to dial her number before, 'was to remind you of Rory's wedding in three weeks' time. You haven't forgotten?'

'No, of course not,' Elexa assured her.

'And Noah will be able to come too?'

Oh, grief! 'Um, I'm not sure. He's very busy—'

'It's on a Saturday,' her mother cut in. 'Surely he doesn't have to work on Saturdays?'

Elexa didn't want to lie to her mother. 'I'll see what we can arrange,' she hedged.

Falling in love had thrown up other priorities, Elexa realised when her mother finally ended her call. Where, at one time, her parent piling on the pressure over some scheme or other would have given her a worrying time, she went to bed that night without feeling stressed over her mother's telephone call, but with her head filled with thoughts of Noah.

Her mother made contact with her several times during the following week, always asking after Noah, but assuming, since Elexa was at her own apartment, that Noah was working out of the country somewhere. With each of her phone calls, however, she particularly mentioned that Rory would feel slighted if she attended his wedding without her husband. Elexa knew full well that Rory would be so absorbed with his bride, Martina, that he wouldn't give a button if neither she nor Noah turned up to wish them well.

By Friday Elexa was starting to feel a degree or two frazzled. She was, as ever, extremely busy at work, though as she loved her job that was no problem.

The problem, she fully accepted, was that she was feeling lovesick for Noah. He hadn't telephoned again, but she hadn't expected him to. But aching for a sight of him, she had lunched at the Montgomery on Tuesday, and had taken a client there again on Thursday. She had sat facing the door, her heart racing each time the door opened, only for her heart to slow down to a dull thud when no tall, dark-haired, grey-eyed, good-looking male came in.

She had decided against lunching there in future. The whole thing was too distracting. Her clients deserved better. In any case, what did she think she was going to do, to say, even if she did see him? What if he didn't so much as nod in her direction? It hadn't been in their contract, unwritten though the contract was, that he had to acknowledge her if he saw her out somewhere.

Elexa, seeing no reason not to, had taken to wearing both her wedding ring and her engagement ring. But it was at that point that the irrationality of being in love took another nip at her. If Peverelle couldn't be bothered to speak, then she couldn't be bothered to wear his rings?

It was at that moment that her sense of humour woke up and she had to smile at how ridiculous her thinking was. Poor darling, she'd hanged him without giving him a chance. His rings stayed on her finger.

On Friday she was on her way to see a client a fifteen-minute walk away from her office. It was a nice day; her meeting was at three. She decided to walk; it would give her an opportunity to get away from her desk and marshal her thoughts.

She did not *have* to walk by the Montgomery restaurant, but, as if to prove that she didn't care if she did see Noah and he ignored her, she just seemed incapable of taking any other route. Not that she would see him, of course, and she wasn't looking anyway.

Determined not to look over to her right as she neared the Montgomery, Elexa looked straight ahead. Noah was probably in the States or somewhere anyhow, and...

'Elexa!'

A voice, a male voice, a male voice she knew, was calling her name, causing her to glance to her left. She halted and scarlet colour flooded her face. Noah, across the pavement from the Montgomery, had been just about to step into a taxi when, turning, he had caught sight of her.

He let the taxi go and came over to her, his glance not missing her high colour as he took in her long length of leg in her well-fitting charcoal-shade trousers, her charcoal-and-white-pebbled tweed fitted hip-length jacket and her long, pale gold-lit blonde hair.

'How have you been?' he asked conversationally, stopping at the side of her, his glance once again on the warm colour of her face.

'Great,' she answered, wanting to laugh with joy—he hadn't ignored her, but had actually hailed her. He looked so wonderful... 'As busy as ever?' she queried lightly.

'Enjoying every minute,' he answered. And then he

smiled, a gentle smile, and she felt that there were no two people in the world but their two selves. But, just when she felt her scarlet colour was starting to subside, he went on, 'At the risk of making you blush again, I think you should be prepared...'

'Prepared?' she queried when he paused.

'It may not have happened—the first time,' he quietly let fall.

She did not at first comprehend his meaning, but she did blush again, scarlet colour scorching her cheeks, as it dawned on her he was saying that it was quite possible that perhaps she had not managed to conceive his child that first time.

With difficulty Elexa strove to live up to her outer sophisticated image. 'You mean we've got to go through all that a second time?' she drawled lazily, and watched as this man she had once thought stern laughed out loud, not at all offended by her reply but very clearly amused by it.

But, as sensitive as she was beginning to know he was, Noah was serious when he quietly assured her, 'It will be better for you the next time.'

She hadn't thought it so very dreadful the first time, but, fearing her ears would burst into flames if she went any redder, she hurried to change the subject. 'You don't fancy coming to my cousin Rory's wedding two weeks tomorrow, do you? I'm sorry,' she apologised at once. 'Cancel that. It was never in our agreement that you, we...'

'You're being pressured?'

'No,' she denied. But, because she only ever wanted to be honest with him, 'Nothing I can't handle anyway.'

Noah looked at her silently for a moment, his expression serious again. Then all at once his expression lightened, and, 'I'd be delighted to come to your cousin's wedding with you,' he suddenly accepted.

He'd be delighted! 'You can't!' she refused, flattening another wave of joy.

'I can.'

'I wasn't being fair in asking you,' she said, but, because everything in her wanted to grab at this chance of seeing him again, her irrational love-torn self added, 'You're sure you don't mind?'

'I'd nothing else planned.'

Oh, Noah. Fearing he might see in her eyes something of the love she had for him, Elexa tore her glance from him and down to watch. 'I've got to dash,' she gulped.

'Appointment?' he asked, flicking a glance to the brief-case she carried.

'Three o'clock,' she answered.

'What time's the wedding?'

'I thought I'd leave about eleven. Shall I pick you up on my way?'

'Your mother would never forgive me if I let you drive me.'

'Shut up,' she said nicely—and they both grinned.

'I'll call for you at ten-thirty,' he said and, bending, he kissed her cheek, and, half turning, hailed a cruising taxi.

Elexa didn't wait to see him get into the taxi, but, looking to neither her left nor her right, she walked smartly on. Had he just done that? Kissed her cheek in parting? She could still feel the imprint of his warm wonderful mouth. Elexa arrived at her appointment with not an idea in her head of what she was doing there—so much for taking the opportunity of that walk to marshal her thoughts!

Pleasurable memories of her unexpected meeting with Noah returned again and again that day. As too did she keep remembering his lovely kiss to her cheek in parting. By Saturday, however, she had seen, as plainly Noah must have done, that their arrangement had gone far beyond a formal shaking of hands.

On the Thursday following, however, Elexa had something else to think about. She was not pregnant. She had not conceived Noah's child—and she didn't know how to tell him.

The fact that he had seen that possibility, and had warned her of it, was of no help. It seemed totally crazy to the logical side of her brain that she could have been so very intimate with him and yet be so shy to tell him what, by the sound of it, he was half expecting to hear anyway.

She spent the weekend growing more and more cross with herself that she couldn't just pick up the phone and tell him. But to do so would mean she was as good as saying they would have to try again. And she felt awkward about doing that. Elexa then started to be cross with Noah too, because, if she did ring his number, there was every likelihood that he wouldn't be at home.

She went to work day after day as usual, often wishing that Desmond Reynolds would go and play somewhere else—the fact that she was now married had made no difference to his flirtatious overtures. Jamie Hodges, on the other hand, while reluctantly accepting that she was married, and therefore no longer available, and while still coming into her office more times than was strictly necessary, had stopped asking her out.

Elexa had still not contacted Noah when the Saturday of her cousin's wedding arrived. I'll tell Noah when I see him today, she decided firmly. This was ridiculous; Noah had to be told.

He called for her as arranged at ten-thirty, and her heart lifted as she could have sworn she spotted a look of admiration in his glance when, dressed in a fine wool suit of burnt orange that brought out the gold in her hair, she opened the door to him.

'Ready, Mrs Peverelle?' he enquired, and she thought him quite earth-shaking enough without him, albeit lightly, claiming her as his wife.

'Yes,' she answered easily, every bit as if she hadn't changed a couple of times before deciding what to wear, and had changed her hairstyle half a dozen times too, before opting to leave it loose about her shoulders.

They chatted about all manner of things on the way to the bride's home church in Wiltshire. But not once was Elexa able to bring up the one subject which she knew she should discuss.

Once at the church, surrounded by her relatives, there simply wasn't any space to discuss anything of such a personal nature with him. He seemed to bear up very well, and even appeared to be enjoying her family when, at the reception afterwards, her mother and her aunts came up and chatted endlessly to him, making sure he felt included in their clan.

They were separated at one stage, and Elexa found she was standing next to her cousin Joanna. 'How's married life suiting you?' her cousin asked.

'Not a single complaint,' Elexa laughed, but, looking at the sleeping Betsy in her cousin's arms, felt the most unexpected maternal pang.

They stayed at the reception until the bride and groom, who were flying off to Tuscany, went to catch their plane. Then, after her family took all of twenty minutes to say goodbye, she and Noah were in his car on the way back to London, and alone again.

They had been driving along for some while when a thought suddenly struck Elexa that she had never previously considered. Noah had once said something about her needing to be numerate in her job. But surely he would need to be numerate in his job too. He must be. Oh, heavens, he was used to calculating, to working things out. Had he worked out that it was about three and a half weeks since that Wednesday she had driven over to his house and had stayed the night? Was he even now waiting for her to say she had, or had not, something to tell him?

Elexa was all churned up inside by the time Noah was pulling up outside her apartment block. 'Noah!' came blurting from her when he cut the engine and looked about to step out of the car.

He turned in his seat to face her, his grey eyes as steady as ever on hers. 'Elexa?' he answered.

'Er—are you—um—around next week?' she asked.

'Huh,' he said, and it seemed to her that in that one short exclamation he was acknowledging that she had just told him that she had not conceived his baby. But she then realised she could be wrong about that, and that he had assumed no such thing, because his voice was quite even when he said, 'I could be.'

She knew then that that was about as encouraging as he was going to get. 'I…' she let go a wound up sigh, and then plunged, 'I—er—need to spend some t-time at your place.' She doubted she would be able to get the words out if he asked her what for.

But he asked no such thing because, as she had only just realised, he was clearly able to work things out for himself, 'Would I be right in thinking that Wednesday might be a right time?' he asked.

'I'm sorry,' she mumbled. 'I feel I've failed you. I…'

'Hey, don't be so hard on yourself,' he butted in. 'You were tense then, breaking through those barriers that were so scary.' He smiled then, and she loved him all the more when he added, 'I believe I suggested that you might not conceive the first time.'

There seemed nothing more to say. Elexa turned to get out of the car and found Noah was ready to open the outer door to the apartments by the time she had found her key.

'Will you have dinner with me Wednesday, or does work have prior claim?' Noah asked as he handed her door key back to her.

But again Elexa, while this time wanting to share as much time with him as she could, didn't think she would be able to eat a thing. She knew, despite having lain with him the one time, that she was still going to be nervous.

'I'll get to you as soon as I can. B-but don't wait dinner for me,' she answered, and, rapidly needing some parting remark, 'Er—thank you for coming with me to Rory's wedding. I...' She was floundering. 'I hope it wasn't too tedious for you.'

'Not at all,' Noah answered charmingly. 'I quite enjoyed being married...' Her heart fluttered wildly, until he added, 'For the day.'

Elexa parted from him without a kiss. After those last three words she was not hanging around for him to be able to salute her in any way. Noah had enjoyed being married for the day—but all too obviously what he was really telling her was that she should not expect anything more from him than that.

CHAPTER SEVEN

ELEXA was glad to get to work on Monday. Yesterday had been so quiet with not one phone call. It was what she had wanted, of course, which made her contrary in the extreme, her mother now having a married daughter she had no need to make plans for, so she had curtailed her phone calls in this, her daughter's honeymoon period.

In all honesty, however, as much as she loved her mother, it was not her voice Elexa wanted to hear over the telephone wires, but Noah's.

Though why he would ring when on Saturday he couldn't have told her more plainly that there was nothing permanent about their arrangement, she couldn't have said. But she had given up trying to cope with the illogical being she had become since Cupid had shot that mighty dart. In any event, she would be seeing Noah on Wednesday; as ever when she thought of driving over to Noah's home on Wednesday, her legs went weak.

'Elexa.' Idris Young had come to see her about a matter he was having a problem with, which gave her something else to concentrate on.

She was grateful to be suddenly swamped with work. Grateful that Tuesday proved to be just as hectic. When, just after four, the phone on her desk rang, as it had been practically all day, she picked it up and said, 'Hello?' more or less automatically, her eyes on the data she had been checking on the computer screen.

'Your husband for you from Brazil,' Faith announced, sounding impressed.

It took all of Elexa's professionalism for her to speak in any sort of an even tone. Noah was in South America! He had given no hint on Saturday that he was going so far away—but perhaps he hadn't known himself, though she had an idea he knew his itinerary months in advance. 'Put him through, please,' she requested, but found that Faith already had.

'Elexa—I'm going to be here longer than I anticipated,' Noah informed her.

'You won't be back Wednesday?' she guessed, disappointment that she wouldn't be seeing him hitting her like a body-blow.

'It will more likely be very early Thursday morning,' he replied.

'Fine,' she answered noncommittally, not knowing quite how to answer but, unsure whether Faith might be monitoring the call, not wanting to give anything away. 'I'll—see you when you get back, then,' Elexa kind of mumbled, aware that her visit to his home had just been cancelled, but while not wanting to end the call, she knew that she should put down her phone.

Only it was not yet over, she learned, when, somewhat obscurely, Noah stated, 'I didn't bring my keys with me.'

'You didn't?'

She was still searching for a clue, when, realising that Noah was equally aware that someone might be listening in, he enlightened her, 'I shouldn't like to disturb you if it's four in the morning when I arrive. I'll get my driver to pick them up from your reception tomorrow.'

Her heart started to race. There had been no question there, but quite clearly Noah was asking her to leave a spare set of keys at Reception for him to let himself in—to her home! He, having just cancelled her visit to his home because he had no idea at what time he would get back, was trying to tell her—without giving any telephone operator who might be listening in a chance to speculate—that he, would visit her.

'I'll—make sure they're there,' she answered as evenly as she could and, so he should know she fully understood, she added, 'I'll see you as soon as you can make it.' Her heart was suddenly thundering, 'Bye,' she said, and quickly put down the phone.

She made a dive for the cloakroom and found she was trembling. But after a few minutes she made herself realise it wasn't her so much whom Noah wanted to see but, having contracted to have a son with her, he did not want to waste another four weeks waiting until her next fertile time.

Which, as she paced the floor in her flat on Wednesday evening, did not make her feel very special. Though why should it? She had gone into this with her eyes wide open. Noah wanted no emotional entanglements, and neither did she. Well, she hadn't until she'd been so crass and stupidly fallen in love with him.

She tried hard to be logical but, love being the brain-scrambler it was, it wasn't easy. She had entered this agreement perfectly aware of what it was all about. She had married Noah for the married status that would stop her mother's almost daily phone calls promoting some man or other—not to mention her mother roping in the rest of the family to assist. She had married him in order to gain some peace to pursue her career and take whatever promotion that career afforded, to pursue her goal and go higher yet higher up that business ladder. All she had to do in return was to give Noah the heir he wanted.

Noah had fulfilled his part of the bargain, and, remembering how he had even attended her cousin's wedding—which hadn't been part of the agreement—he had fulfilled his part magnificently. Now it was up to her to fulfil her part.

Around midnight Elexa decided to go to bed. She had given serious thought to sitting up and waiting for Noah. But, in a snatch of a logical moment, knew she had an extremely busy day planned for tomorrow, and Noah had mentioned the possibility of it being four in the morning before he arrived. Perhaps if she could get a few hours' rest before then?

She had some vague notion that planes were not allowed to land in London before five in the morning but, considering that she rarely flew anywhere, what did she know? Besides, for all she knew Noah could be flying in on some private jet and landing anywhere.

Realising that big, big business was vastly different from the big business she was in, Elexa showered and got into bed. She put the bedside light out, then realised that, since Noah did not know the layout of her bedroom, perhaps it would be better if she left it on. Not that she expected to go to sleep for a moment.

She awoke with a start, opening her eyes to see Noah standing there. 'I'm sorry,' he apologised softly, 'I didn't mean to wake you.'

'I didn't mean to go to sleep,' she answered. She sat up and went to get out of bed, had a belated moment of modesty when she remembered the thinness of her nightdress—but asked anyway, 'Can I get you something to drink? A sandwich?'

'I had something on the plane. I wouldn't mind a shower, though.'

While Noah took his bag with him to the bathroom Elexa made room for him in her bed. It wasn't as large as his bed, more a three-quarter than a double. But at least it wasn't a single.

'H-how was business?' she asked when he returned. He was wearing a robe, but appeared to be wearing little else, and she was suddenly feeling nervous—and trying not to show it.

'Hectic, but satisfying,' he answered, and, coming to one side of the bed, began to untie the belt of his robe.

Hurriedly Elexa looked away, and the next she knew Noah was getting into bed beside her. He was close, the bed too narrow for there to be any real kind of space between them.

She lay down, his naked skin burning through the thin material of her nightdress. 'You look tired,' she observed, though not actually looking at him. 'Would you like to sleep a little f-first?'

'First?' he queried, on a low laugh, then reached for her. He turned her to face him, the length of their bodies touching. She knew then that he was not too tired to make love to her. 'Still scared?' he asked, planting a light kiss on her mouth.

She kissed him back, and as she felt the need of his body, so a need for him started to stir in her. 'Not scared, exactly,' she answered honestly. 'It—lovemaking—is still a bit new.' She voluntarily kissed him. 'I have, after all—' she smiled '—only ever tried it once.'

'Now there's an invitation if ever I heard one.' Noah smiled back at her and, so saying, gathered her more closely to him, and, his head coming down, he kissed her. Gently he parted her lips with his own, his hands a whisper of tenderness as he caressed her slowly closer to him. And as her need for him began to soar, so Elexa wanted to be closer, ever closer to him.

'Noah.' She moaned his name when his sensitive fingers teased the hardened peak of her breast.

Again he kissed her, then pulled briefly away from her

to put out the light. 'Are you going to let me do the honours this time?' he teased softly, his fingers already busy with her nightdress.

She laughed, a tender, loving laugh, and just loved and loved him, when at last naked with him, Noah tenderly took her to new and yet more thrilling heights.

Elexa was an early riser, but that Thursday morning it was nearing seven-thirty when she opened her eyes. Any other morning and she would have leapt out of bed to try to catch up on her late start to the day. But that morning she was not in bed alone.

Noah's rhythmic breathing told her he was still fast asleep. As she thought of how exhausted he must have been from his travels and yet how, out of consideration for her, he had not hurried his lovemaking but had taken time and care in case she should experience any stray stand of discomfort while he introduced her yet more fully to this new and wonderful world, such an infinite feeling of tenderness washed over her that she wanted to gently hold and kiss him. He had said that their lovemaking would be better for her that time and, thanks to his unimagined sensitivity, it had been.

Elexa then began to grow more and more aware of the feel of his warm naked skin against her own, and a fresh wave of need for him washed over her and began to mingle with her feelings of tenderness. That was when, quietly taking the greatest care not to disturb his exhausted form, Elexa got out of bed.

For the first time ever as she silently moved around, bathing and getting dressed, Elexa had a sensation of not wanting to go to work. She had the oddest notion that she wanted to stay home, perhaps cook breakfast for Noah, maybe spoil him a little…

For goodness' sake! Abruptly she put the brakes on all

such thinking. Even so, even telling herself that Noah would think her a loony if she tried any such thing, Elexa was in the hall, briefcase in hand, when she had the almost undeniable urge to go into the bedroom and take another look at Noah. She had no idea when she might see him again.

Love was the most weakening emotion, she had discovered, and it took all her powers of determination to walk out of her apartment. Only the thought What if he was awake? spurred her on to move. She drove to her office, knowing for sure that, had Noah been awake, he would be interested in neither her cooking him breakfast nor in her having a go at spoiling him. He was a businessman, was Noah, and the instant he was awake he would be up and about his business.

Around mid-morning she started to worry that he might have some meeting he should be attending. Perhaps she shouldn't have left him sleeping. But he'd only had a few hours' sleep, the love she bore him argued. But work is work, and he loves his work, argued her business head.

So she rang her home number, and there was no reply, and she knew then he had left her apartment, that he wouldn't be there when she got home that night—and she so wanted him to be there.

The weekend came and went, with her mother telephoning her once and suggesting that, with things unusually quiet on the family front at the moment, perhaps she and Noah would like to come to dinner one evening. 'Of course, I know you're still enjoying being newly married, so I don't expect you'll want to come too soon,' she added, then, going on, 'Poor you. Noah must be away again or I wouldn't have found you at your place.'

It was a fact that Elexa had no earthly idea where Noah

was. He could be on any of the continents as far as she knew, or even in London.

On Thursday in the week that followed she had lunch with her old friend Lois, but was mercifully saved from answering more than a query of how was Noah with a smiled, 'Fine,' because Lois had a new man. What Hugh thought, did, ate and drank seemed to fill up most of the lunchtime.

Elexa did so wish that Lois's new relationship would work out. But a week later Elexa had a fresh worry of her own. She discovered she was not pregnant and spent the weekend feeling dreadful because it was so.

By Sunday she was feeling a complete and utter failure. She knew she had to let Noah know; she had left it too long to tell him the last time. She rang his number in the morning; he wasn't in. She tried again in the afternoon. By evening she was searching for some way to phone his PA on Monday to try and find out where he was, without letting Gillian Owen know that Noah had a very unusual marriage in that his wife had no idea of his movements!

Elexa had one last try later on Sunday evening, 'Peverelle,' he answered—and her heart seemed to leap straight out of her body.

'It's—it's Elexa,' she managed.

'Something worrying you? You sound—quiet?' he said.

'I'm—um…' She tried again. 'It didn't happen,' she said. And, when he was the most astute man she had ever met, just in case he hadn't understood, she explained, 'I'm not p-pregnant.' Silence was her answer. He's cross about it, she realised, and that plus her guilt at feeling a failure caused her voice to proudly sharpen as she told him, 'Naturally we'll divorce…' My word, if she did!

'We'll divorce when I say we'll divorce!' he rapped

furiously before she could take another breath. 'And not until then!'

'I...'

'You made a bargain with me,' he snarled through anything she might have been trying to say. 'You have your side of the bargain, a marriage to keep your family quiet,' he reminded her hostilely. 'How dare you think for an instant to try and back out of our agreement? I won't—'

What he would or wouldn't, Elexa did not wait to hear. She put down the phone, her ears singed enough, thank you very much. She was offended too. She'd had no intention of trying to back out of their agreement!

Elexa had cooled down from her anger by the following day, but still wasn't certain that she wouldn't have ignored Noah Peverelle had she passed him in the street. There was no sense in this love business, she mused, not for the first time—how could she make such wonderful love with him and yet be quite prepared to stick her nose in the air should she see him?

A couple of days later and Elexa was aching for a sight of him again, and had completely forgotten that she had been minded to walk straight on by should she have seen him while out and about.

But she didn't see him. Not then anyway. Although she had just finished her evening meal on Thursday, and was thinking about taking a look at some work she had brought home with her, when the outer buzzer sounded. She went to answer it, 'Hello?' she enquired—and nearly collapsed in shock.

'Noah,' replied a superb, well-remembered voice.

Noah! Her heart raced and her throat went dry. Noah was here! Noah was here. Overjoyed, Elexa was about to press the button to let him in when her pride—which hadn't been too visible since she had fallen in love with him—decided to give her a prod, and abruptly she was recalling the snarling way he had spoken to her when she had phoned him on Sunday.

'Don't tell me you've forgotten your key!' she fired sharply, only then remembering that he still had her spare keys.

'I wasn't sure of my reception,' he replied and, when she didn't want to laugh, her pride slunk away, and Elexa felt her lips twitch.

'You'd better come up,' she invited soberly, and didn't wait to hear what he answered—probably nothing, knowing him, but pressed the button to let him in. She had just time to run and pull a comb through her long blonde hair before Noah was ringing her doorbell.

She loved him so. All she wanted to do was open the door to him and throw her arms around him. She opened the door—how marvellous he was. He was business-suited, so she guessed he had just left his office. He studied her in turn, his fine grey eyes taking in each dainty feature.

'You're over your rotten temper, I hope,' she said for starters, tearing her gaze from his quite fabulous mouth.

'I should have counted ten,' he owned. It wasn't an apology, but she supposed it came close.

'Come in,' she invited, and when he followed her into her sitting-room, she offered, 'Can I get you a coffee or something?'

He shook his head. 'This won't take long. I—'

'You've changed your mind? You *do* want a divorce?' she cut in, pride rearing its ugly head again.

'No, I do *not* want a divorce! Hell's teeth, woman,' he barked, checked, then took a steadying breath. 'Shall we sit down?' he suggested.

Elexa thought it a good suggestion and took the chair nearest to her, while he took the one opposite. But looking over at him, loving him so very much, she just didn't want to fight with him and, before she knew it, she found she was explaining—apologising—and making a very good job of it. 'I wasn't trying to get out of our—um—bargain,' she told him swiftly. 'I'm sorry if you thought I was. It was—well, you know I thought I'd failed you when I—er—it didn't happen before. This time I was feeling a double failure… And I suppose I thought *you* would want a divorce because we d-don't seem to be getting very far.'

Noah surveyed her for long moments. Then, suddenly, he smiled. It was a nice smile, a giving smile, and Elexa fell in love with him all over again. 'You're too anxious,' he said softly, and because his tone, his smile, was making a nonsense of her, Elexa had to force herself to concentrate on guessing why he had come to see her. It wouldn't take long, he'd said, and it wasn't about divorce. So why…? Colour flared to her cheeks as she realised that Noah must have calculated that next Wednesday would be the right time for them to try for a baby, but had called to tell her that he had to be elsewhere at that time.

'You're going to be away next Wednesday?' she blurted out in a rush, very much aware of Noah's speculative glance on her heightened colour. 'You needn't have called; you could have said over the phone,' she added just as speedily. 'You—'

'I am home,' Noah interrupted.

'You are? You're not going away?' she questioned, more slowly this time.

'For a change, I shall be in London all next week,' he informed her.

'That—um—*will* be a change,' Elexa commented. 'But…' bearing in mind he had never called to let her know his whereabouts before '…that wasn't what you came to tell me?'

'It wasn't,' he agreed, and paused for a moment before he revealed, 'The fact is that I've been batting off strong hints for weeks now that you and I spend some time with my family.'

'My mother would quite like it if we had dinner with them at some future date, too,' Elexa mentioned, to let him know that she understood.

Noah gave her a friendly look which warmed her heart, and went on, 'Naturally I've got the two of us out of anything specific.'

'Naturally,' Elexa murmured, intelligent enough to know that that wasn't the end of it. 'But?'

'But now Lewis Wheeler has proposed to my sister, and Sarah has accepted.'

'Oh, how lovely!' Elexa exclaimed without thinking.

'Oh, it is,' Noah agreed. 'Except for the fact that Sarah, probably because she has been engaged and married before, doesn't want an engagement party this time.'

'Am I allowed another but?'

'You are,' Noah permitted, and Elexa felt a warm glow. 'But,' he continued, 'my mother is still feeling short-changed that you and I didn't have an engagement celebration.' Elexa had had no idea of that, and warmed to him some more because, whatever family pressure Noah had been under, he had handled it without worrying her with it. 'I'm afraid that not only is she insisting that Sarah at least has an engagement dinner—but is insisting that I'm there too.'

'Ah!' Elexa exclaimed, and thought she had it, but asked anyway, 'Where do I come in?'

'You're my wife,' Noah answered succinctly, and Elexa's whole being leapt at the joy she felt to hear him say those three words.

'You want me to come with you?' she asked, her voice

remarkably calm in the circumstances—his wife, she was his wife, and she was to spend some time with him!

'Would you mind?'

'After you so nobly came to my cousin's wedding with me? I wouldn't dream of refusing,' Elexa replied sunnily. Though suddenly a thought struck her. 'We wouldn't have to…? I mean, we're not staying the night? I know it's a drive of an hour or more, but—' She broke off, feeling awkward all at once and wishing she had never raised the subject.

'You know I don't snore,' Noah answered pleasantly, but there was such a gleam of devilment in those grey eyes that Elexa knew that he was teasing.

'In that case, I won't bother to take an overnight bag.'

Her concentration on the job at hand the next day was at a minimum. Again and again her thoughts kept winging to tomorrow, and the hours she would spend with the man she loved.

'How's my favourite flower?' Des Reynolds stopped by her office to enquire.

At one time she would have acidly rebuffed him. But today she barely noticed him. 'Blooming,' she answered, and discovered that her soft dreamy tone had far more effect than any sharp instruction that he go play on the motorway.

'You love another,' he accused.

She saw no reason to deny it. 'True,' she answered— and he went off in disgust.

There was one area in her workday, however, where she had to concentrate her thoughts: when her immediate boss came and told her that the vacancy for a junior manager would be posted on the staff noticeboard later that day.

'Should you intend to apply—and you'd have my backing—I'll miss you, Elexa,' he added.

Elexa was ready and waiting when Noah called for her late on Saturday afternoon, and she stored up every wonderful memory of that drive down to Sussex. It seemed impossible then—as she and Noah sometimes chatted, sometimes were companionably silent for long stretches, and then talked some more, even laughed together occasionally—that she had ever thought of him as being stern.

'What sort of a week have you had?' she asked him once.

'The usual juggling of hours,' he replied. 'How about you? That promotion you're after any nearer?'

'The managerial position?' She was flattered that he had remembered. 'The vacancy was officially announced yesterday.'

'You've applied?'

'Clive hinted I should.'

'Clive?'

'Clive Warren, my immediate boss.'

'Sounds as if the job's yours,' Noah deduced.

'How do you make that out?'

'Either Clive Warren wants to get rid of you from his section, which I don't believe for a moment,' Noah replied, 'or he's going to recommend you for the post.'

Elexa felt all gooey inside that Noah didn't believe Clive wanted her out of his section. 'Clive said as much,' she admitted.

'So you did apply?'

'I think mine must have been the first application in.' She smiled. 'Though, since there's a closing date, I shall have to wait ages for my interview.'

'You'll get it—the manager's job,' Noah said, and sounded so positive about her abilities that she wanted to hug and to kiss him for his confidence in her.

She and Noah were warmly welcomed by Ruth and

Brandon Peverelle, and Elexa quieted any feeling of guilt that she and Noah weren't the 'normal' married couple, as perceived by Noah's parents, by consoling herself that, as Noah had said, she was his wife. She did love him too. And, since Ruth Peverelle was very like her mother, and might be as anxious also for a grandchild, perhaps with any luck she would be able to present them with their first grandchild before too long.

'I've given you Noah's old room,' Ruth Peverelle was saying as they stood in the hall. But, just as Elexa was starting to feel a touch panicky, she realised that Mrs Peverelle had very kindly merely given them Noah's old room perhaps in case she wanted to freshen up, or, if she'd arrived wearing jeans, wanted to change before dinner.

Just then, however, Debbie, who had come to give a hand in the kitchen, appeared, and seemed to have need of an urgent word with their hostess. 'I'll show Elexa up,' Noah volunteered, and together they went up the stairs.

Only halfway up, Elexa suddenly halted. 'Perhaps I should have offered to help,' she spoke her thoughts out loud, half turning to go back the way they had come. But Noah, taking a hold of her elbow, stopped her.

'The more I know you, the more I'm charmed by you,' he remarked, his expression serious as he looked down into her eyes. Her heart turned over with joy. But she guessed she should take that as no more than a passing compliment for, in the next moment, Noah was giving her elbow a little nudge to urge her on their way and was commenting conversationally, 'Trust me—my mother will have everything well organised and will have all the help she needs. She can handle a special dinner for seven without turning a hair.'

Noah showed her to the light and airy room that had been his in his growing years. Elexa wanted to touch the furniture his hands had touched, to lie on the large bed on which he had once lain, a bed that had probably been changed from a smaller one as he had outgrown it—then realised she was going all soft inside about him again.

'Seven?' she picked up rather belatedly. She had some-how gained an impression that, because Noah's sister didn't want any fuss, it would be just the six of them at dinner.

'Sarah didn't think it fair that Lewis should be outnum-bered by the Peverelle's—she invited his brother along.' Having dealt with that subject, 'The bathroom's through there,' Noah said, pointing to the other door. 'My father wants to show me his latest engineering gadget.'

She wouldn't have minded looking at the gadget either, but it was probably an all-men-together type of thing. 'See you later,' she said pleasantly, aware that it wasn't so much the gadget she was interested in as a need to spend every moment she could with Noah.

You've got it bad, my girl, she lectured herself once Noah had gone. We have an agreement, pure and simple, and it is never going to be anything more than that, so get that indelibly printed in your brain, do. Hadn't Noah that day of Rory's wedding said it plainly enough? Noah might have hinted at being briefly charmed by her, but that didn't alter the fact that once she had given him the son he wanted it would be divorce time. 'I quite enjoyed being married,' he'd said, but, to let her know there was nothing permanent in their relationship, so she needn't start think-ing otherwise, 'For the day' he had added.

Because she did not want to be in the way, should it all be happening on the catering side, Elexa stayed upstairs until Noah came looking for her. By then she'd had an injection of pride that declared Noah Peverelle could go hang if he thought for a moment that she wanted it any other way. A divorce would suit her just fine.

'Did I do something?' he enquired as they went down the stairs.

Trust him to notice that her mouth smiled but that her eyes did not. 'Of course not,' she denied at once, and was glad that there was no chance of other private conversation because by then they were crossing the hall to the drawing-room.

It was obvious that Sarah and Lewis were ideally suited and the evening got off to a good start with everyone toasting them with champagne.

Because this was a special time for the newly engaged couple—their evening—Sarah and Lewis were the focus of attention. But as they all moved to the dining-room, so Ruth Peverelle managed to have a private word with Elexa.

'I'm so glad you were able to make it this weekend,' she beamed, 'and so happy that Noah found you. You'll make a big difference to him.' She gave her arm a small squeeze. 'You'll have to use your influence to stop him working so hard.'

Aware that her influence was nil, all Elexa could do was smile and take her seat next to Noah.

Scott Wheeler, Lewis's brother, was somewhere in his late twenties and, although not as tall as Lewis, he was good looking and, Elexa discovered, full of chat. He was sitting at the other side of her at dinner and, because she intended to take jolly good care that Noah knew nothing of the depth of the love she had for him, she was happy that Scott chatted to her. His conversation was inconsequential, but at least it gave her something else to fix her thoughts on other than the man she had married.

Quite when during the meal she became aware that Noah was displeased about something, she couldn't have said. Perhaps he wasn't displeased about anything at all, she tried to tell herself. Perhaps, over-sensitive where he was concerned, it was just her *over-sensitive* imagination *imagining* it.

It was towards the end of the meal—Sarah and Lewis and their future plans being the centre of attention—that Sarah, having frequently brought her future brother-in-law into the conversation, turned her attention on to her obviously adored elder brother.

'So you're home for a while, Noah?' she asked.

'Just next week,' he answered.

'Then you're off where?' his mother joined in.

'Europe, mainly.'

'Didn't I hear you were off to Australia?' his father asked.

'Next month,' Noah replied.

'Are you going with him, Elexa?' his mother enquired.

I should be invited! 'Not this time,' Elexa answered.

'Oh, what a pity! But you'll be able to go to Vienna with him when he addresses that major international conference?' Ruth Peverelle persisted. 'Noah will be so thrilled to have you there, at his most—'

'Elexa has her own career,' Noah chipped in pleasantly.

'Yes, but...' she began, but was interrupted by her husband.

'It's not for six or seven weeks yet, dear,' Brandon Peverelle reminded her with a smile, and it became obvious to Elexa that Noah's parents followed their son's career with loving parents' natural great interest. 'And as long as Noah is there—' he turned to smile at his daughter-in-law '—that's the essential thing, isn't it, Elexa?'

'Of course,' she answered gratefully, not knowing the first thing about it, though as the talk went on she started to glean that, come hell or high water, Noah, as chief speaker, had to be there.

'What sort of work do you do?' Scott Wheeler butted in to ask her, and Elexa, while extremely proud of Noah's achievements, was so relieved to be off the subject of the important international conference in Vienna of which she was supposed to know something but of which in actual fact she knew nothing, that she gave Scott a warm smile.

'I'm with Colman and Fisher, the marketing company,' she replied, and, out of courtesy, asked, 'What sort of work do you do?'

Elexa listened agreeably to his reply and then rejoined the general conversation which, thankfully, was back with Sarah and her fiancé.

Elexa stayed talking with the two of them for quite some while, until they adjourned to the drawing-room. But the whole of the time she could not lose the feeling that something had upset Noah. He was as calm as ever, as polite and affable as ever to his family, clearly great friends with his father—but still that feeling persisted.

She was in the middle of laughing at some absurd story Scott Wheeler was telling her when she caught Noah's sharp glance on her. She was still endeavouring to decipher what, if anything, that sharp look meant and, amusing though Scott was, quite ready to go home, when the party began to break up.

But, when Elexa was ready to make her goodbyes, she was the one to be upset when, before she could so much as thank her hostess for a wonderful meal, her hostess was beaming. 'You seemed a little light on luggage, Elexa. If there's anything you need, just ask.' She smiled. 'If you're comfortable this time, you might stay longer next time.'

'We're not—' Staying, Elexa would have said, given the chance.

'Often free,' Noah cut in smoothly. 'But we'll make a note of it,' he added, and smiled, said a general goodnight to everyone—and took Elexa firmly by her upper arm and steered her to the stairs.

Elexa had been extremely well brought up but knew, without being taught, that it was just not done to make a scene when you were a guest in someone else's home. However it was touch and go in the next couple of seconds that she did not shake Noah's hand from her and march straight to the front door.

By the time they reached the room—Noah's old room— Elexa was seething. Though she did not have to shake his hand from her, because the moment the door was closed Noah took his hand from her and, from the sudden angry glint in his eyes, Elexa guessed that he was as furious as she. Though what he thought he had to be furious about, she couldn't fathom.

Whatever, she wasn't waiting for him to tell her, but pitched straight in. 'You *knew* we were staying!' she accused hotly.

'I specifically said that we weren't!' he grated.

Much good that had done! 'You could have got us out of it. When you—'

'Why should I?'

'Stop butting in!' she ordered. 'Why shouldn't you?'

'What's the matter? Want the chaste little bed all to yourself?'

'You're sleeping in that chair!' she hissed, pointing to a quite well-padded bedroom chair—which looked for all its padding as if it might be hell round about three in the morning.

'Where else?' he grunted.

'Good,' she sniffed, and, that established, she charged

into the bathroom and closed the door with a determined click.

She was still fuming, but as she noticed that in between now and the last time she had been there Mrs Peverelle had had fresh toothbrushes and toothpaste put in the bathroom, so some of Elexa's anger started to fade. Ruth Peverelle dearly loved her son and didn't see nearly enough of him. Wasn't it only natural that she would want him to stay?

Elexa went slowly back into the bedroom. Noah did not seem to have moved, but was standing more or less where had had last seen him. 'Why are you so mad at me?' she asked.

'You were mad at me first,' he replied, looking stern again, though—and she wasn't so very sure—she had an idea he was not so annoyed with her as he had been.

'You sound ten years old,' she accused.

'So what did I do? You were all uptight with me earlier.'

'When?'

'When I came to take you down to dinner,' he reminded her.

'W—' She broke off, remembered, and suddenly felt forced into honesty. 'I'd been having a silent argument with you,' she confessed.

He looked intrigued. 'I don't appear to have come off best.'

It all seemed so ridiculous now, but honesty would out. 'The argument went along the lines of—Who did you think you were, being happy to be married to me—for a day? That's what you said when you dropped me off at my place after Rory's wedding. By the time you came up for me tonight I was in a We'll-divorce-any-time-you-like-pally kind of mood.'

She felt stupid confessing that, and about the ten-year-old she had accused him of being. But she was little short of amazed when, after staring at her for long, silent mirthless seconds, Noah suddenly burst out laughing. 'Oh, Elexa Aston-Peverelle, did I mention that I had never, ever met anyone like you?'

'So,' she murmured, loving him to the roots of her being, but striving not to let it show, 'I shouldn't have let it tweak my pride?'

'And I shouldn't have objected that you all but gave Scott Wheeler your telephone number.'

Elexa stared at him in astonishment. 'I did no such thing!' she protested, it occurring to her for one heart stopping moment that Noah might have been jealous!

'You told him where you work.'

'Anyone could have told him that.' Suddenly she was aghast. 'Did I miss the signs?' Noah didn't answer. 'You don't think…? He wouldn't…?' All at once she saw that it was nothing to do with jealousy but the pride Noah had too. Noah had been annoyed that she, missing whatever signals Scott Wheeler had been sending, had laughed and chatted with him, and had believed, in front of his nearest and dearest, and had been angry in that belief, that his wife was giving some other man leave to contact her.

'I do, and he will,' Noah answered her unfinished questions. 'What are you going to do when he gives you a call on Monday?'

She smiled, and then laughed, and as Noah's glance went from her eyes to her mouth, and then back again to her laughing eyes, she answered, 'Well, naturally, I shall refer him to my husband.' Her laughter, her smile, started to fade as Noah stilled and then just stood staring at her. 'What?' she asked. 'What's wrong?'

Noah seemed to give himself a mental shake. 'Nothing,'

he replied, and was smiling. 'Other than you're one rather delightful lady.'

Her breath caught, not only at his words but at the warmth in them. But steady on here, she cautioned, and found another smile. 'You're still sleeping in that chair,' she informed him.

His smile had gone into hiding. 'I—want to hold you,' he said.

Her heart leapt—she wished he would. 'Not a good idea,' she answered, fighting with all she had the urge to run to him.

'You're right, of course,' he agreed—but came a step nearer.

It was her cue to take a step back, but she was hungry for his arms about her, and found she had taken a step forward. Then he was reaching for her and, shyly, unprotesting, she went into his arms.

As he had said he wanted to, he just held her quietly to him, held her quietly against his heart. It was bliss, wonderful, heart-easing bliss, to be there in the strong circle of his arms. She placed her arms around his waist, loving him so much, breathing in his warmth, and rested her head against his chest.

How long they stood like that, just wrapped in each other's arms, she had no idea, no sensation of time. It was just too, too perfect. Soon, it would end. Soon, she knew, Noah would step back from her and let her go.

Pride struggled to get a hold. He mustn't know how she felt about him. She stirred in his hold and raised her head to look at him. Now he would let go of her.

But first he bent his head and placed a gentle kiss to the side of her face—and she didn't want him to take his arms from around her. 'That was—um—nice,' she said huskily, and wanted to ask for another.

Then found that she had no need to ask because, whether he read the request in her eyes she had no idea, but Noah smiled, a gentle smile, and placed his warm mouth tenderly against the other side of her face.

She wanted to tell him that was nice too, but rather gathered he knew she had no objections because his head came down again, and this time he placed a gentle kiss on her waiting lips.

'You're a very heady woman,' he murmured softly against her mouth.

If she was heady, she didn't know what that made him! She wanted another kiss and, pride or no pride, she didn't seem to have the power to resist. Their lips met again, gentle still, but his hold on her was firming.

He kissed her again, and she gloried in his kisses. When Noah pulled her that little bit closer to him, she involuntarily pressed nearer to him.

She heard a small sound of wanting escape him, and was glad, because she wanted him too and had to swallow hard when he placed his hands in the blonde thickness of her hair, burying his head in her hair, kissing her neck, her throat.

Then his lips found hers again, parted them, tasting their sweetness, and his hands caressed down to her spine, one hand caressing round to her right breast. 'Oh, Noah,' she whispered shakily. And with what little intelligence she had left, 'W-we shouldn't be doing this,' she reminded him, knowing that he knew as well as she that this wasn't her fertile time—and that they had no excuse for kissing each other.

'We shouldn't?'

'It's not in the charter,' she whispered.

'I know,' he admitted, and shrugged out of his jacket in order to get that bit closer to her.

Again he kissed her, drawing a very fire from her. She wanted to cry his name again, but his lips had taken charge of hers once more. She felt the tender touch of featherlight kisses over her face, then felt his sensitive fingers busy with the zip of her dress.

Slowly he moved her dress from one shoulder, tracing tender kisses over her silken skin. A tinge, a mere tinge of shyness caused her to clutch at him when her dress fell from her shoulders, but he held her to him until that moment had passed. The next time he kissed her she seemed to slip her arms out of her dress without knowing it, the same way she stepped out of it and allowed Noah to scoop it up and place it over a chair—and she was in his arms again, receiving and giving as their lips met.

'Th-this should stop,' she mentioned huskily, having never stood in front of a man in her underwear before, and suddenly taken by more shyness.

For answer, Noah smiled down at her. 'Tell me to stop, and I will,' he replied.

Oh, she couldn't bear that. 'That's a rotten thing to say!' she admonished huskily—and he laughed, a wonderful joyous laugh.

'My darling,' he breathed, and, kissing her, he gathered her against him.

Willingly she pressed into him, new sensations, even more fiery sensations taking her as she felt his hands on the firmness of her behind.

She loved him, she wanted him, wanted to feel his skin against her skin. In a sudden fever of wanting to know his skin once more, she raised her hands to his shirt buttons—his tie, along with her tights, had gone some minutes before.

Gloriously they kissed, and as Noah allowed her the freedom to remove his shirt, so she allowed him the freedom to remove her bra. 'Sweet love,' he breathed, his words, his touch, thrilling her as he pressed her throbbing naked breasts into his broad naked chest.

More minutes passed as, with his hands again on her behind, he pulled her against him, passion soaring as he kissed her breasts, taking one hardened pink peak into his mouth, kissing, tasting, nibbling—and as fire rocketed through her, Elexa wanted to do the same to his.

She stroked the dark hair on his chest, caressed his chest and, when she could, caught his nipples in turn gently in her teeth. She was on fire for him, as she knew he was for her, and she reached up and kissed him, and when at last Noah broke that kiss, it was to draw back to gaze his fill at her naked breasts.

'You're so very beautiful, my darling,' he murmured. 'I just have to kiss your delicate skin.' So saying, and starting first with the sweetness of her lips, he tenderly kissed her throat, her breasts, and, removing her last remaining garment of clothing as he went, proceeded to kiss her belly and her thighs, causing her to gasp in pleasure.

Then she was in his arms again and his mouth was over hers and he was lifting her, carrying her over to the bed and pulling back the covers, was gently laying her down.

He left her briefly to put out the light, and she urgently wanted him back with her again. So urgently, eagerly wanting him back with her that as he reached for her, so she reached for him.

He gathered her in his arms once more and lay down with her, and as their legs entwined she knew that he had removed the remainder of his own clothing, his skin burning against her skin as they pressed naked together.

'Noah!' She cried his name as, his touch exploring, growing more and more intimate, he took her to still yet more new heart stopping unexpected heights. 'Noah! Noah!' She wanted him beyond bearing.

'Shh, my darling,' he soothed her, but she guessed he knew how much on fire she was for him, because lingeringly he deeply kissed her, passion leading him too as she arched yet nearer to him. As she abandoned herself to the utter joy of soon being as one with him she almost screamed out, in the storm of her need for him, that she loved him. She did not know why she didn't. All her other inhibitions had gone.

CHAPTER EIGHT

'YOU'VE gone all dreamy eyed again.' Idris coming into her office unexpectedly on Monday, caught her out.

She dealt with his query speedily and efficiently, but the moment he had gone she was back again in the wonderland of Noah's lovemaking on Saturday. She had never experienced anything like it. Only now, now that she knew what true passion was like, was she able to realise how very much Noah had been keeping himself reined in the other two times they had made love.

She loved him all the more because, out of consideration for her innocent body, he had been so gentle with her and had taken time to... Hastily Elexa pulled herself together and got on with some work; this would never do! But her time with Noah on Saturday had been so incredibly shattering, within a very short time, she was again marvelling with wonder things about herself she had never dreamed existed. She recalled the feeling of utter liberation when, Noah's touch doing mind-bending things to her, her hands of their own accord had wandered off to rove, to explore, to caress and stroke his superb body. She had obeyed the overwhelming need to feel his skin and been encouraged by his passionate reaction to her sensitive searchings.

The passionate joy they had found together still astonished her. She had eagerly clung to Noah, crying his name, wanting more—more of his kisses, more of his ardent caresses, more of his endearments.

'My darling love' he had called her when, at the height of their shared passion, she had met his fire with an unsuspected matching fire of her own. Her desire for him burning out of control, holding him with urgent, wanting hands, she had felt the joy and urgency of his touch, responding with her all as Noah took her to new, and yet more new and staggeringly unexpected pinnacles of rapture.

Tenderly, when passion had been spent, Noah had kissed her face, such tenderness taking the place of the inferno of fire that had consumed them both. 'You were bewitching,' he breathed. 'An unimaginable delight.'

Elexa lay in the dark looking up at him, still in the thrall of his lovemaking. 'I—never knew it could be like that,' she whispered. 'I—never knew *I* could be like that.'

He tenderly touched his lips to hers, and she loved his kisses, loved his body on hers. Loved the intimacy of it, the freedom. Noah seemed to like it too. 'Sweet enchantress,' he murmured. 'But you must get some rest.' And she wasn't sure he did not sound regretful as he moved from her. But intimacy was still there when Noah bade her, 'Go to sleep,' and tenderly kissed her breasts, kissed her mouth again, and kept her in the cradle of one arm until she slept.

She opened her eyes at some time in the night and felt his body-warmth against her, and everything inside her collapsed in a loving jumble. She loved him so much. Did he perhaps love her a little? Don't be stupid, scoffed common sense. Love was never part of the bargain. She halted on that thought. Neither had to make love when there was not the smallest chance she would become pregnant been part of the bargain. Hope rose—and she gave herself up to the bliss of just lying beside the man she loved.

She fell asleep again, but was awakened by someone knocking on the bedroom door. It was Noah's mother, to tell him he was wanted on the telephone. Some flap or other going on.

He was instantly awake, or perhaps had already been awake, but he had one arm still around Elexa when he called, 'I'm on my way,' to his mother. Though he seemed in no hurry to start his day. Sitting up and looking down at his wife, he apologised softly, 'Sorry to wake you.'

'Good morning,' she bade him shyly.

'You can blush like that after what you did?' he gently teased.

After what she did? He had been the instigator! 'I—er—your phone call's waiting.'

He sighed heavily, then grinned at her, but, unconscious of his nakedness, got out of bed, his back to her. Instinctively she closed her eyes, but he was her husband and last night she had enjoyed his body to the full. It seemed ridiculous to start being modest now. Elexa opened her eyes again. She loved the tall, long length of him as he found his clothes and shrugged into them.

She thought he would go without another word, but he came back and sat on the edge of the bed. 'All right?' he asked, looking into her velvety brown eyes.

Never better. 'All right,' she answered.

'That's my girl,' he said, and bent and kissed her, followed that kiss with a gentle smile—and then went to take his phone call.

Elexa stayed where she was after he had gone. She didn't want to get up. Perhaps Noah would come back. Perhaps he would take her in his arms again. Perhaps...

Wondering what Noah had awakened in her that she should want to be in his arms again, to make love with him again, Elexa speedily got out of bed. Her underclothes were strewn around the bedroom and she quickly gathered them up, grateful that Mrs Peverelle had merely knocked on the door and had not popped her head into the room to tell her son of his urgent phone call.

Elexa was grateful, too, for Noah's thoughtfulness in hanging her dress over a chair, and went to take a quick shower. She was dressed and had just finished tidying her hair when Noah returned.

'Do you always eat breakfast?' he asked, coming to stand behind her, their eyes meeting in the mirror.

'Only in the potato-picking season,' she replied, and absolutely adored him when he kissed the top of her head.

'I have to return to London,' he informed her.

She gathered that meant straight away, and was already on her feet. 'Well, grab me a King Edward and let's go,' she responded.

Their goodbyes to his parents were hasty. 'Come and see us again and stay longer next time,' Ruth Peverelle instructed, giving her a hug. Noah's father gave her a hug too, and as soon as they had said goodbye to Sarah and Lewis, they were on their way.

'Scott must still be in bed,' Elexa murmured as the car sped northwards.

'He didn't stay overnight,' Noah stated, and after an unsmiling moment asked, 'You know what to tell him when he rings you at your office?'

She didn't think for a second that Scott Wheeler would do anything of the kind and could not take Noah's question seriously. 'Yes, dear,' she said obediently, as any good wife would. She didn't think Noah was going to be amused, but, glancing at him, she saw his lips twitch.

All too soon they arrived at her apartment building. Noah got out of the car with her and, looking down at her, 'I'll be in touch,' he said, and as brown eyes stared solemnly back at him he drew her to him and kissed her. He stepped back, his gaze still on her, and she desperately wanted to know what he was thinking. But, without another word, he turned swiftly away and went smartly back to his car.

Elexa went home from work on Monday and waited anxiously all evening for the telephone to ring. It did not ring, and Elexa, having been up on high, because of some absurd notion that her time with Noah over the weekend might have meant a little something to him, plummeted down to the depths because all too obviously it hadn't.

Perhaps he was extremely busy, she excused him, when she awoke on Tuesday. After all he had needed to rush back to London on Sunday.

Reading the newspaper in her lunch hour, Elexa discovered what Sunday's flap had been all about. Some well-known company was attempting to take over one of the companies under the umbrella of the Samara Group and had yesterday received a brief answer for their trouble. International Chairman, Noah Peverelle, had apparently politely advised them that, in the unlikely event of Foskett and Williams coming on the market, he would personally let them know. In other words, don't hold your breath.

Noah did not telephone her that night either, and Elexa started to become increasingly anxious. Her fertile period had begun yesterday and would end Friday. The very best possible chance she had to conceive his child would be tomorrow, Wednesday. He knew that; she knew that he did.

She got up on Wednesday, certain that Noah would ring that day. He had phoned her at work before, so he knew where to get hold of her. She went home that evening with the only personal call she had taken being from Scott Wheeler, who had telephoned to say he was in the area and could he take her to lunch?

Elexa had been feeling so heartsick waiting for Noah to

ring that she'd felt like telling Scott she'd love to have lunch with him and could he make it the Montgomery? Two things had been against that. It had only been a very remote possibility that Noah would be lunching there today and, anyway, she had no wish to encourage Scott Wheeler.

So she had given him the answer any respectable married woman would. 'I'm sorry,' she had apologised nicely, 'but most of my lunch hours are taken up with business— and those that aren't I reserve for Noah.'

Bad form, Elexa—prim—she mused as she put down the phone. She could have been kinder. On the other hand, Scott had got a nerve. Be it only lunch he'd invited her to, it was still the thin end of the wedge. But, anyhow, she was off men in general at the moment.

Her phone rang when she got in. She made a dive for it. It was her mother! 'I thought you must be there. I rang Noah's place first, knowing he was in England, but there was no reply.'

'Noah's a bit busy this week,' Elexa invented off the top of her head.

'I know. He was on television at lunchtime—something fascinating to do with finance. You'll be going over to his place later, I expect?'

'Mmm.' Which wasn't an outright lie. 'How are you— and Dad?'

Apparently her mother hadn't phoned for anything in particular—it just seemed to her an age since they had last spoken, and she chatted away for ten or so minutes before saying, 'Well, I mustn't keep you. Noah might be trying to get through as we speak.'

Since Noah was not trying to get through, Elexa wondered if she was supposed to ring him. Hang that for a game of marbles! He *knew* today was *the* day. If he couldn't ring her, she'd be blessed if she would ring him.

She went to bed that night wondering, since Noah still had her spare keys, if he might let himself in later. Bubbles to that, she thought, and started to get angry. Yet, even angry, she hated herself that, because she loved him so much she couldn't be sure she would definitely tell him to get lost, should he turn up in the middle of the night.

By morning she was feeling defeated. She still loved him, even though she wished that she didn't. She had wondered why she had not told him of her love for him when last Saturday they had made love so fantastically. She now knew why. Noah did not love her. True, she quickly reminded herself, it had never been in their agreement that he should love her. But she had so hoped that their time together last weekend had meant something to him, however small.

But all too clearly it hadn't. If anything, it seemed as if he had gone off her. Ah! Suddenly her breath caught and she felt as if she had received a blow to her heart. A gasp of sound escaped as it all at once came to her that last Saturday's spontaneous lovemaking had taken Noah by surprise. It should not have happened but it had, and, despite his parting 'I'll be in touch', he obviously would not be. Noah Peverelle, the man she had married, had clearly stated in her hearing that he did not have space for any emotional entanglements. Clearly, when for once their lovemaking had been unplanned, the fact that she had responded so wholeheartedly had him running scared.

By the time she was showered and dressed, Elexa was ready to punch his head. After a night spent in torment, frantically worrying if she had given away her feelings for him in those heady unplanned moments, she drove to work looking at everything from another angle.

Just a minute, here! Who did he think he was? What right had he *not* to phone her? Him, with his 'My darling love'! It wasn't *all* her fault, or even half of it. *He* had been the one to start it! Let him ring now—she knew he was in the country; her mother had seen him on TV.

He did ring. After the dullest weekend Elexa could ever remember, Noah rang her on Monday evening. Her heart leapt the moment she heard his voice, and she promptly forgot every thought she'd had about what she would tell him when and if she ever spoke to him again.

'It occurred to me that perhaps I'm not being entirely fair,' he commented for openers.

'Fair?' she queried carefully; as yet she had no idea what this call was all about, but was well aware that he knew that her fertile time was now over.

'To your parents,' he answered.

'I'm not with you.'

'We've spent time with my parents since our marriage,' he replied—when she had been certain *that* weekend would never get a mention. 'It seems only right, as your mother has suggested we have dinner with them some time, that we spend some time with your parents.'

Good heavens! Feeling very much staggered—and, she had to admit, warmed by this turn of events, Elexa just had to check her hearing. 'You want us, you and I, to go to my parents for dinner?'

'I thought if there's a restaurant near to them you'd recommend, maybe we could take them there. I have to be away tomorrow for a few days. But if next Saturday is convenient for you and them…?'

'I'll see what I can arrange,' Elexa said, and, realising she should perhaps have hedged a little, 'I'll give you a call towards the end of the week,' she added, and hastily put the phone down before she might agree to anything else that might be on offer.

Not that he would be suggesting anything else, she

scolded herself firmly. It was only his sense of fairness that had him contacting her now. That, and perhaps a thank-you to her for going down to his parents' home the other Saturday… Oh, for goodness' sake, don't start thinking about that time again. Not that it was his lovemaking she dwelt on so much, more their wonderful kind of togetherness, the feel of his strong arm about her as she surfaced from sleep. The…

Elexa was in bed that night when, with a start, she all at once thought she had the answer to why Noah hadn't contacted her last week. He wanted a divorce.

She felt as if she had been kicked, winded, when she suddenly saw what all this was about. That Saturday night they had shared at his parents, unplanned, unscheduled, had been a mistake. A mistake that had caused him to reconsider the wisdom of staying married.

Quite plainly, in his re-evaluation of his situation, he had decided to end it before matters became any more entangled. And, she all at once realised, in making that decision he, having this 'thing' about fairness, was just evening up the 'parental' score. She had dined with his parents; he, in turn, would dine with hers.

Elexa went to work the next day ready to tell Noah Peverelle she had no interest in his 'fairness' of mind. There was no way she was going to contact her parents and invite them to dine with them.

That evening, her mother rang, and Elexa found that she didn't have any choice in the matter. 'I thought, as Noah has to go away again, that I'd give you a call in case you were feeling lonely,' her mother almost sang, and before Elexa could begin to wonder how her parent had known he was away, she said, 'Noah rang me this morning, as you know.' Kaye Aston rattled cheerfully away. 'I told him about the Royal Oak Hotel being so good, and he said he'd book it for Saturday.' She chatted on in the same vein, plainly believing that Elexa had known all about Noah's morning phone call. 'I'm looking forward to seeing you both again,' she stated happily. 'I'm so looking forward to Saturday.'

What could she say? 'So am I,' Elexa replied, and spent some minutes after her mother had rung off intensely disliking Noah Peverelle. It didn't last, of course. She went to bed as deeply in love with him as ever.

'You were going to ring,' he reminded her when he telephoned on Saturday morning—he would never know the effort of will it had cost her not to ring him.

Just hearing his voice made her feel all weak, and she found that, when she'd vowed no word of apology was going to pass her lips, she was saying, 'I'm sorry. I must have misunderstood. I thought I was to phone you to tell you what I'd arranged. But I believe you've already done the arranging.'

'You're annoyed with me?'

Oh, Noah, don't do this to me! 'Who could be annoyed with you?' she answered lightly.

'So I'm allowed to call for you at six-thirty this evening?'

'I shall be ready and waiting,' she promised, and loved him, loved him, loved him, and if this dinner tonight was a prelude to divorce, she didn't care—she simply ached to see him again. She spent the rest of the day wondering what to wear.

'You look terrific!' Noah smiled when she opened the door to him—and he bent and placed a kiss on her cheek.

For a man about to propose divorce, the kiss to her cheek was unexpected. Her heart danced a little jig all of its own as, dressed in a cream funnel-necked fine wool suit, her long legs shown to advantage in an above-the-knee skirt, Elexa went with him out to his car. When it came to terrific, he wasn't too bad himself.

'Busy week?' he enquired once they were on their way.

'Happily so,' she replied, glad to be busy—if only to escape the torture of her thoughts. 'No need to ask if you've been busy.'

'I suspect we both thrive on having busy lives. Have you heard about your interview yet?'

'The closing date for all applications is a week next Friday, so I won't hear before then.'

'You'll get it,' he assured her.

She loved him! 'Don't tempt fate!' she implored.

He laughed. 'I've every faith,' he said, and chatted easily most of the way to the Royal Oak Hotel.

They arrived at around the same time as her parents, and the evening went along splendidly. So much so that, for a short while, Elexa even forgot her certainty that Noah would be mentioning the word 'divorce' before too long.

Then she remembered, and felt a little panicky that he might say something about getting divorced in front of her parents. Noah asked, 'Are you all right, Elexa?'

Oh, my word. She quickly found a smile. 'Of course,' she answered, not for a second prepared to let him into the bleakness of her thoughts, or her panic either, but not missing that her mother was all smiles that her son-in-law seemed to be most concerned for her daughter's welfare.

All the way on the drive home Elexa waited for Noah to tell her—duty done, fairness dealt with, the score once more even—that now was the time to talk divorce. But he did not, and she was sure—having had her nose bitten off once and being accused of trying to back out of their agreement for daring to mention it—that she wasn't going to be the first to bring it up.

'I've enjoyed this evening,' Noah commented formally when he saw her to her door.

'So have I,' she answered, as any nicely-brought-up girl would.

'Goodnight,' he bade her, and, bending, he kissed her, and was too quickly gone. She went indoors—not quite certain how she felt about the evening. She had loved seeing him, but somehow everything seemed unsatisfactory.

The plain truth, she mused as she lay waiting for sleep to come, was that she didn't want any dutiful light kisses in parting from her husband. She wanted to be held by him, and to be loved by him. Not particularly sexually, she just wanted him to love her—but she might just as well cry for the moon.

Life went on, she found, when a week followed of her being extremely busy. She managed to find time to lunch with Lois on Monday—Lois still being heavily involved with Hugh—but Elexa worked through her lunchtime for the rest of the week, and worked late most evenings.

She had just arrived home on Friday when the man who occupied her every free space for thought rang. 'I was rather hoping I might be able to see you tomorrow,' Noah began, and Elexa felt sick inside—there was only one thing he wanted to see her about.

'Oh, yes?' she replied pleasantly, just as if she hadn't a clue that it was divorce time.

'But there's a weekend conference I can't get out of.'

Divorce, obviously, could be put on hold. 'Well, you know how much you enjoy your work.' She hung on to her pleasant tone.

'Where were you Tuesday?'

'Tuesday?' she enquired, startled at the bluntness of his question.

'I rang—you weren't in.'

'Oh,' she murmured, feeling all over the place, not knowing if she was glad or sorry she hadn't been in—love was truly making a nonsense of her. 'I was working.'

'Until ten at night?' he questioned sharply.

Get him! She might be married to him, might love him with everything she had, but she still had charge of her own life—or thought she had. 'A girl has to eat.'

'I could have met you when you finished—taken you for a bite.'

It saddened her that he was so keen to end this marriage he'd have met her when she finished work to discuss it. 'I went and had some dinner with a friend.'

'Not Lois?'

Part of her thought he was fishing to know whom she had dined with, but the sensible part of her knew that Noah, being a private kind of person, he didn't want her friend Lois knowing that while he was still in the country his wife wasn't rushing home to him.

'I went with Gary, one of the team,' she answered.

'I'll give you a ring when I get back,' he said crisply. 'Goodnight.'

'G...' she began, but he had already put down his phone. Swine! she fumed, and loved him so much it was almost like a physical pain. The next time he contacted her would be to arrange to see her so he could tell her that he wanted their marriage ended. Sad, but true.

Elexa heard not a word from him in the week that followed, and the waiting started to get her down. She felt physically sick sometimes, just thinking about it. So that by the time Friday came round again she didn't think she could take much more of the waiting.

In a weak moment she tried to cheer herself up by considering that perhaps she had got it all wrong. Perhaps for some reason—some reason with a simple explanation that

Noah would tell her about if she asked—he hadn't been able to contact her during her last fertile time. Perhaps next week, when her fertile time came round again, Noah would ring to...

When the next week her telephone was deafening by its silence, Elexa knew that she had not got it wrong. Noah did not want a son with her. That much was now blatantly obvious...underlined, and chiselled in stone.

A dry sob escaped Elexa as she faced that she could say goodbye to any last remaining doubt that Noah was regretting their marriage. He must be regretting it wholeheartedly.

Had he not been, this would have been the week when they should have tried again. Knowing that she was still fairly new to this sort of calculation, on Sunday Elexa idly checked her workings out. She was as numerate as Noah had suggested that she had to be in her job, so she knew she had no need to check again her cycle of what should happen and when—she was just filling in this gaping void. She picked up her pen and began ticking off...and abruptly stopped dead, nearly fainting with shock!

Everything in her went haywire as she made herself go back to the very beginning and start to recalculate afresh. Then she just sat utterly stunned. Because in her recalculation of the various dates of what should happen, and the dawning realisation of what had not happened, Elexa suddenly knew that there was no need any longer for her to work out when it was best for her to conceive because—she already had!

She was pregnant! She couldn't possibly be! That Saturday at Noah's parents' home... But—she couldn't be! It wasn't possible! She must have the dates all wrong.

Deny it though she might, and try to believe she had to have it all wrong, there was no doubting the test she did

as soon as she was able to purchase a pregnancy testing
kit the next morning. The test proved it—she was having
Noah's baby!

Gradually over the rest of the day Elexa started to get
her head back together. Instinctively she wanted to tell
Noah at once. But that was when she recalled that Noah
had gone off the whole idea of being a father—otherwise
he would have been in touch. She had to accept that, while
he had never wanted a wife in the accepted sense, he no
longer wanted to be a father either.

By Friday Elexa knew conclusively that Noah had gone
off the idea of having a son. He was a business man who
by and large must live by his diary. He must have
known—since he had no idea she had made a mistake in
her calculations—that last Wednesday should have been
the best time.

She slipped out of work early on Friday afternoon, feeling extremely well but also feeling so completely ignorant
about what she should or should not be doing to safeguard
her baby, that she went to see her doctor.

Elexa returned to her office feeling highly emotional that
her doctor had confirmed she was having Noah's child.
She had realised through holding Joanna's baby that she
did have a little maternal feeling, but Elexa discovered that
she so wanted this baby that, when Clive Warren came
into her office and told her the glad news that she had an
interview next Thursday for the junior manager's job, she
was hard put to be as enthusiastic as she would normally
have been.

'Great!' she beamed, but the inner glow she felt had
nothing whatever to do with that chance of promotion
which she had worked so hard towards.

She awoke the next morning feeling glad that it was
Saturday and that she didn't have to go into work.

Because, in contrast to how extremely well she had felt yesterday, that morning she had barely put her feet to the floor than she was diving for the bathroom.

Her bout of morning sickness lasted until about lunchtime. By four that afternoon she was feeling her old self again. Then her phone rang. She thought it wouldn't be Noah—but it was.

'Sorry I haven't been in touch,' he apologised.

'You've been busy, I expect?'

'You could say that. Working in overdrive,' he answered, adding, somewhat obscurely, 'All means to an end,' and, before she could decipher that, 'Any chance of you having dinner with me tonight?'

Her heart began to pound. She could tell him about the baby—her heart slowed—he could tell her about their divorce. 'You're lucky,' she said lightly. 'My engagement book shows a clean page for tonight.'

She thought there was a smile in his voice. 'I'll call for you,' he said, and rang off.

She went down to meet him that night, and he was as she remembered him—wonderful. What he was thinking she had no idea, but she had a notion there had been an admiring look in his eyes the moment before he'd kissed her cheek in greeting. Then, taking her arm, he guided her over to his Jaguar.

Her spirits lifted—was that the look, the action, of a man who wanted to end their agreement, a man who wanted to divorce? She had been torn all ways ever since his phone call. Everything in her urged her to tell him about the baby—he had every right to know. But would he *want* to know?

The restaurant Noah took her to was small, expensive-looking and intimate. 'Gin and tonic?' he queried while they sat studying menus. 'Or would you prefer wine?'

'G…orange juice, please,' she remembered in time—she fancied a gin and tonic too.

Noah's glance showed interest, but he allowed her to make her own decisions without questioning her, and ordered the orange juice—with no idea that it would be better for his baby than the gin Elexa would have preferred.

'Hungry?' he enquired.

Having been unable to fancy much in the way of food that day, Elexa suddenly realised that she was starving. 'Ravenous,' she confessed, and decided there and then that she would tell Noah that evening about the baby. He would have to know anyway. It was his right.

She started her meal with a pear in tarragon sauce, and was just tucking into her second course of a succulent piece of salmon with delicious vegetables when she was aware of Noah looking at her.

'Am I pigging it?' she asked, suddenly self-conscious.

He smiled. 'It's a joy to see you eat,' he answered blandly. 'So many women merely pick.'

She almost confessed then that she was 'eating for two', but she was side-tracked by the niggling thought of him eating with 'many women'. 'You've been overseas again?' she asked instead.

Noah looked solemnly at her. 'I was in Australia the week before last, and I've been out of the country for a few days this week,' he agreed, then paused, and deliberately stated, 'But I was in London all of last week.'

'I—see,' she said slowly, and promptly lost her appetite. If Noah had not been in England last week then he had every excuse for not contacting her last Wednesday. But, had he wanted to let her know just how very much he did *not* want a baby with her, then he could not have put it more plainly had he told her outright.

She looked him straight in the eyes then. They had al-

ways before only ever been honest with each other.
'You've gone off the idea of having a son, haven't you?'
she asked.

Noah gazed steadily back. 'Let's say that, recently, I've
begun to think it wasn't the best idea I ever had.'

Recently? As in, after that weekend down at his parents'
place? She was hurting, but she smiled. 'If I remember
rightly, I approached you out of the blue.' Pain cut deep.
'By the way—' she abruptly changed the subject '—isn't
it next week that you're making that speech to some conference in Vienna?'

'Next Thursday,' he agreed. 'Elexa, I—'

'What time?' she asked.

'My speech?' She nodded. 'Some time around four, I
believe.'

'I shall think of you,' she said lightly. 'At precisely four
o'clock next Thursday,' she babbled on, 'I shall be being
interviewed for that promotion I—'

'The promotion to junior manager? You'll get it,' he
said, sounding as certain of that as he had before.

'Not that it's as important as what you'll be doing,' she
reminded him modestly.

'Don't say that. I know how important this promotion
is to you.'

'Well, you're right there,' she agreed, trying not to feel
stunned at the thought that suddenly arrived from nowhere:
that her baby was perhaps more important. 'Come fire,
flood or high water, I shall be there for that interview.'

'On your hands and knees if you have to?' Noah teased,
and she loved him.

'It's as important as that to me,' she confirmed with a
smile. 'Nothing short of a major disaster would keep me
from attending.' And, having coped with her hurt that,
without any question of a doubt now, Noah was not inter-

ested in being made a parent, 'But I imagine you feel pretty much the same about what you have to do next Thursday?'

'Pretty much,' he replied with an answering smile. He paused then, before he added, 'I've a full day on Friday too, but after that I'll get back on Saturday, and plan then to have more time for me.'

'No more gallivanting all over the place?' she somehow managed to tease.

'Somebody else can do it.'

That surprised her; she had thought he loved it. 'You've had enough?' she queried seriously.

'There are other things I want to do,' he answered.

But having a child, being a father, isn't one of them, Elexa thought sadly, and, having said she was too full for a pudding, a short while later they left the restaurant and Noah took her back to her apartment.

She did not invite him in; she saw no point. Nor did he ask to come in, or even hint as much. He, equally, she realised, saw no point. 'Best of luck in Vienna,' she bade him with a cheerful smile.

'I won't wish you luck with your interview—you'll get the job,' Noah stated as, almost toe to toe, they stood at the outer door of her apartment building.

There seemed nothing more to be said. 'Goodnight,' she said quietly, suspecting that nothing would ever be the same between them again.

For answer Noah gathered her into the circle of his arms, and she had a moment's hearts-ease when he held her close up against him. 'Goodnight, my dear,' he replied softly, dropped a light kiss on to the top of her head—and went striding away.

Elexa climbed the stairs to her flat, choking back tears. She loved him so much, but that kiss just now...it was almost as if he had said it, as if it had been no more than an It's-been-nice-knowing-you-but-what-we-had-is-over kind of kiss.

Elexa went to bed and lay there wide awake and trying not to cry. But she had never felt so wretched, and a few tears did escape. Were it not for the baby, she would never see Noah again.

Given a choice she would prefer not to tell him at all, but knew that some time, though perhaps not for a month or two, she would have to tell Noah about his baby. She knew for certain that she wouldn't be able to keep it from her mother for too long. Which meant that as soon as her ecstatic mother knew, she would most likely be on to the other set of soon-to-be grandparents. Elexa couldn't do that to Noah—let his parents inform him that he was to be a father.

Having thought she had never felt so wretched, Elexa went to get out of bed the next morning and the floor came up and hit her. She felt dreadful as, clutching onto furniture, she made it to the bathroom. She eventually staggered out again with her intelligence telling her that this wasn't just a queasy tummy—this was morning sickness with a vengeance.

So much for 'morning' sickness, it stayed all day. She fell into bed that night exhausted and, while not wanting to be a nuisance at the doctor's surgery, she needed to know if she should be feeling this ghastly. She also needed to know if her baby was all right. From nowhere, she was suddenly feeling fiercely protective.

The next day was no better, but she struggled into work. She visited her doctor later in the day and was assured that all was well. Her doctor offered to prescribe something to help, but Elexa decided she would get through without it, and returned to work. But for the first time ever she watched the clock. Promptly, at five, she went home to bed.

Her doctor had said it would soon pass, but the next morning, and the next, it took all of Elexa's power of will to stay vertical. How soon, she wondered, was soon?

'You look awful!' Carol exclaimed, coming in to the cloakroom on Wednesday and catching her after another wave of nausea.

'Stomach upset,' Elexa explained.

'Why don't you go home?' Carol urged.

It took a tremendous effort of will, but Elexa managed to find a smile. 'Never,' she answered.

She awoke on Thursday morning and was afraid to stir. She did not want to get up and felt so tired it was as if she had never been to sleep. Carefully she slid her legs out of bed and gingerly stood up—and it started.

The bathroom seemed to have become her second home, but eventually she was able to stagger back into her bedroom. Today was the day of her interview—oh, grief. She had to be bright and alert—and she felt like death. She had to smile, answer intelligently in-depth questions, and find some intelligent questions to ask of her own—and all that was in her head was the hope that she didn't have to dash out of the boardroom to part with whatever sustenance she had thus far managed to hold down.

Fortunately she had a wardrobe full of smart business-like clothes, so pulled out the nearest to hand. But by the time she was dressed and ready she was already running a half an hour late. She was still feeling groggy when she went to the door of her apartment. She was halfway through the door when a stray waft of someone cooking bacon for breakfast finished her.

Knocked sideways, Elexa made it to the bathroom—just; nausea such as she'd never known was in charge. She spent the next ten minutes recognising she had never ever felt so ghastly—or so miserable. She wanted her mother. She wanted someone to come and take charge. She wanted someone to make her feel better.

But most of all she wanted Noah—and Noah was in Vienna, getting ready to make that most important speech. But, anyway, even if he wasn't far away in another country, he wouldn't want to know.

Suddenly nothing mattered. Not her job, nothing. She staggered to her bedroom without sufficient energy to get undressed, and collapsed on to the bed, fate laughing hollowly. So much for her telling Noah at the outset that she could easily cope with pregnancy. Her pregnancy was in its early stages yet—and already she was breaking her never-had-a-day-off-work-sick record!

Elexa surfaced some while later and summoned up sufficient energy to dial the offices of Colman and Fisher to say she wasn't feeling well.

'For you not to be feeling well must mean you are really laid low, particularly on a day like today,' Clive Warren said, sounding very concerned. 'Have you called your doctor?'

'I've seen her,' Elexa replied, but, wanting nothing more than to put the phone down and to get some sleep, 'I'll be in tomorrow,' she promised.

'You stay exactly where you are until you're feeling better. I'll do what I can about your interview.'

Elexa lay down again the minute the call had ended. She closed her eyes but was awakened just after midday by the ringing of the telephone. Immediately she thought of Noah—and could have wept because she always did think of him. Only it wouldn't be him—it would never again be him. Why, for goodness' sake, would it be him? He was too busy preparing for that speech he would give at four o'clock to so much as give her a thought—besides, as far as he knew, she was at her office.

She did not want to talk to anyone, and was glad when the phone finally stopped ringing. She dozed off again and awakened just after two, trying to convince herself that she felt better.

For the baby's sake she forced down a couple of biscuits and drank some water. Tomorrow, she promised, she would really get herself sorted out. If she couldn't eat breakfast or lunch, she would make up for it in the evening. Just thinking of food sent her reeling to the bathroom again.

When later she seemed to have an ounce more energy, Elexa thought she might feel better if she freshened up a little. To that end she cleaned her teeth and got out of her clothes. Then she took a brief shower and got into a fresh nightdress. After which she felt so exhausted again she went back to bed.

She glanced at the clock. Just coming up to four. Noah would be about to start his speech. Oh, how she wished she could be there with him. Oh, how she wished he could be here, with her. She loved him so much. Already she loved his child. She also knew that, whatever agreement they had made in the past, or would make in the future, she did not want to be parted from their baby.

Elexa was suddenly consumed by a feeling of anxiety. He wouldn't take the baby away from her, would he? Could he? She didn't know. She felt sick again. Then was startled out of her panic and misery to hear the door of her apartment being quietly opened!

She wanted to get up and run, to barricade herself in from the intruder. But she felt paralysed, and could do nothing but, her eyes enormous, stare at the door as the handle began to slowly turn. *Someone was entering her bedroom!*

Helplessly, her heart thundering, Elexa stared at the door. Stared as it slowly, quietly, opened further. She had thought she was about to faint from the knowledge that she was in no fit state to do battle with the burglar. But, as a tall, dark-haired, business-suited man stepped in through the open doorway, Elexa felt she would faint from shock!

Her heart didn't merely thunder as he quietly closed the door and began to approach her bed, it thrashed about violently. 'Noah!' she gasped—and felt certain she must be hallucinating.

CHAPTER NINE

HER eyes were enormous as Elexa watched Noah come closer to her bed. 'W-what are you doing here?' She managed to string a sentence together as she struggled to sit up in bed.

'I might ask you the same question,' Noah replied evenly, his tone controlled as his stern glance raked her ashen face.

'Y-you're—supposed to be giving a speech—right now,' she mumbled, feeling totally bewildered and half ready to believe she really was hallucinating. Was Noah *really* here?

'And you're supposed to be having an interview for a job you prize more than anything,' he reminded her, his keen grey eyes taking in the dark shadows beneath her eyes. 'What's wrong, Elexa?' he asked quietly, kindly.

She didn't want him being kind—it melted her backbone, and she needed all the stiffness she could find. 'Nothing's wrong!' she denied, and knowing that there was only one reason why he had come to see her, albeit that she was utterly confused wondering why he had chosen a time when he should be elsewhere, addressing some vast conference, 'You've come to discuss our divorce,' she stated wearily.

She caught his look of astoundment, quickly hidden though it was. 'Are you delirious?' he questioned.

She wondered that herself—he shouldn't be here, but he was. 'Why else would you be here?' she asked.

'I'm here because Clive Warren said—'

'Clive Warren! My boss?' she exclaimed. 'What—'

'I rang your office.' Noah forestalled her question and, coming closer, his eyes still fixed on her, he sat down on the edge of her bed.

Good heavens! Surely he wasn't that keen to get divorce discussions started that he had rung... 'Where did you ring from?' she questioned abruptly as the thought landed.

'From Vienna,' he answered, his eyes never leaving her face.

'You rang my office from Vienna?' She was having difficulty taking it in. It was of no help to her powers of comprehension either that, as the shock of seeing him so unexpectedly started to recede, Noah should be sitting so close to her.

'I thought I'd wish you luck with your interview after all,' he replied.

'Oh, Noah,' she said softly. 'That was kind of you.'

He shrugged that away. 'Only you weren't there. Someone said you were off sick.'

'Ah,' she mumbled.

'So I rang here...'

'Was that you?' she exclaimed. 'Around midday?'

Noah took on board that she had been in, had heard the phone ringing, but had obviously decided not to answer it. 'When there was no reply I rang your mother...' Her eyes shot to his in alarm, until he continued, 'And tactfully discovered you weren't there.'

'She'd have had a fit if you'd told her I was off work sick but that you couldn't find me!'

'That's what I thought, so I rang Clive Warren for more information.'

Noah had made two calls to Colman and Fisher! When he was so very busy, he had taken time out to... 'Oh, Noah, I'm so sorry I put you to all that trouble.' It sounded as though he had been quite worried about her. But surely he hadn't quit the conference purely on her account! Ridiculous. She didn't believe it. Though—he wasn't due back until Saturday. He had told her that only last Saturday.

'Warren said you were ill. In his view you must be extremely ill—you'd never taken so much as half a day off for sickness in all the time you've worked for the firm.' Noah paused, and then quietly asked again, 'What's wrong, Elexa?'

'Nothing, honestly,' she replied, aware that her lie didn't look good, not with her nightdress-clad and sitting up in bed at four o'clock in the afternoon.

'Nothing that is so bad you've called a doctor in to see you?'

'I didn't call a doctor in—I went to see one,' she quickly contradicted.

'And this was because there is nothing wrong with you?' Noah took up, starting to sound tough. 'Look at you, your eyes as big as saucers, not a scrap of colour in your face, your...'

'I'm feeling much better,' Elexa assured him hurriedly, and, given that she wasn't yet ready to test her feet on the floor, and given that she was feeling extremely anxious, she realised she was feeling better than she had all day. 'I've rested all day,' she told Noah truthfully, 'and...'

'Are you in pain?' he questioned urgently.

'No. Not at all,' she denied swiftly.

'What does your doctor say is wrong with you?' Noah wanted to know.

Elexa racked her brain for some minor ailment. She wasn't flushed and there wasn't a sign of a cough or a cold about her. 'Women's problems,' she brought out of thin air, and felt certain that would kill that particular line of enquiry. But—it didn't.

'What sort of women's problems?' Noah seemed determined to know. Stubbornly, she refused to answer. 'This is the first time you've ever had to take time off work because of them,' he pressed.

She didn't want this conversation. He was getting close. She should never have said 'Women's problems'. What had she been thinking of? 'Please—drop it, Noah,' she requested huskily.

'How can I, my dear?' he asked gently. 'I know how very vital this promotion interview is to you. Yet suddenly, when everyone seems to know you are never ill, you are too ill to attend.'

Elexa stared at him and loved him so much. He had to know about the baby, she knew that he did, but not yet—she needed time to think. She had only just discovered herself how much she wanted to keep her baby, and while Noah had begun to think the idea of him being a father was not the best idea he'd ever had, she wasn't ready to take the risk of Noah deciding she must stick to their initial agreement and hand the baby over to live with him.

'I'm fine, Noah, honestly,' she lied.

Her hands had been resting on the coverlet and his answer was to reach forward and take both her hands in his. 'That's what your big eyes and white face are all about, are they?' he probed gently, and she wished he wouldn't use that gentle tone—it weakened her, causing her to feel all emotional and weepy.

'I'm fine,' she repeated, in panic lest she should cry all over him. 'And—and there's no need, no need at all, f-for you to be here,' she said in a rush. 'I...' She ran out of steam, and felt exhausted suddenly. 'Oh, Noah!' she wailed.

In the next second she found he had moved nearer to the bed head and, sitting next to her, had reached for her and was cradling her in his arms. 'What is it, my darling?' he crooned against her ear.

'D-don't be nice to me—I'll be in tears.'

'Oh, we can't have that,' Noah decided, and, for all the world as if he needed to get closer to her, in the next few seconds he had shrugged out of his jacket, removed his tie and shoes, and was sitting alongside of her on the bed, once more gathering her into his arms. 'Now, tell me all about it,' he murmured against her hair—and Elexa came closer than ever to blubbering all over him.

'It was kind of you to phone,' she said, swallowing hard and making a determined effort.

'Why wouldn't I?' Noah asked, holding her to him with one arm while stroking her hair back from her forehead with his other hand. 'My best girl was about to go through an interview that meant a great deal to her.'

His best girl! She knew he was teasing her because she looked so washed out, and that he was being teasing and kind from the sensitivity she had witnessed in him. 'B-best girl,' she repeated, liking the sound of that so much. 'C-could we be friends, do you think?' she found she was asking, feeling better than she had in an age to have him there with her, to be held quietly in the curve of his arm.

'I do so hope so,' Noah answered, and Elexa loved him all over again because, at the end of all this, perhaps they might be friends. 'Hmm, any particular reason why you'd like us to be friends?' he asked casually, and if she didn't know better she might have thought he was fishing for something.

She knew she was going to have to be careful. It surprised her that he hadn't picked up on her slip with regard to 'women's problems'. Though perhaps—since he was convinced she was numerate and no huge problem for her to calculate when she was likely to conceive, or likely not to conceive for that matter—that she might be pregnant was just something it wouldn't occur to him to consider.

'No reason, other than—um—well, we have been—er—close,' she said, and, feeling her colour rise, went on quickly, 'And—er I have grown to like you.'

Noah adjusted his position so he could see into her face. 'That's a very good start,' he commented, his eyes on her. 'Oh, sweetheart, you do look a wan little waif,' seemed to be jerked from him, and, as if he couldn't help himself, he placed a tender kiss on her forehead.

'That's no way to speak to a respectable married woman,' Elexa replied, needing some light remark in her fear she would cry at his amazing tenderness with her. She accepted then that she was in a highly emotional state.

'Forgive me,' he smiled. 'You see before you one very worried, respectable married man.'

'Worried?'

'About you.'

'Oh, please don't be worried,' she pleaded, and nearly told him then and there that all that was wrong with her was that she was pregnant with his child. But that protective maternal something—newly-born in her—held her back. 'T-tell me instead that you like me a little too,' she said instead, and was instantly appalled at what she had just said, and added hastily. 'You don't have to, I...'

'Not even if it's true?' he asked, and smiled.

'Well, yes. In that event, then yes.'

'So it's true,' he said softly. 'I suppose I must have liked you almost from the beginning.' And, his tone gently teasing, 'Despite you telling me you'd rather marry a man-eating shark than marry me.' She laughed, and she gathered that had been his aim when he gave her an encouraging smile. 'Then I found that the more I knew of you, the more I started to like you,' he added.

Her heart started to leap about. She loved the tender way he was looking at her, even if she did know that he was only being like this with her because he thought she was ill. 'D-did you?' she asked, and suddenly knew that, before he left her flat—as he probably would at any time now— she would have to tell him what her 'women's problem' was.

'I did,' he agreed. 'In fact, I liked you so well on our wedding day that when we walked back up the aisle together I felt enormously proud to have my beautiful bride on my arm—' He broke off, and then added quietly, 'In fact, that day I began to experience emotions that were totally new to me.'

Elexa stared at him, her heart drumming *and* leaping. 'You didn't want anything to do with emotions,' she reminded him shakily.

'Neither did I,' he admitted, and as if he couldn't resist it, he said, 'You're starting to look a little better than you did,' and gently kissed the corner of her mouth. 'So there was I, emotionally proud to stand beside you while we posed for wedding photographs. And later, when I dropped you back here and kissed your cheek, like so,' he murmured, pausing to kiss her cheek, 'I discovered I was emotionally enchanted by your lovely laughter-filled face.'

'Oh,' she sighed, and his arm around her tightened— almost as if he intended to protect her for ever. And she so wished it was so, and not mere whimsy of thought on her part.

'Little did I know then that a whole barrage of emotions were hiding around the corner, just waiting to trip me up,' Noah confessed softly.

'Honestly?' Elexa queried. Perhaps they really could be good friends. Never had she expected Noah to open up like this.

'Totally honestly,' he replied. 'First I was furious with you that you had never made love with anyone before, then I was emotionally all over the place that I was the only one—and emotionally all over the place in Germany the next day, when the memory of your sweetness the night before kept coming between me and my work.'

'No!' she gasped, having thought nothing came between him and his work! Though, to give the lie to that, what was he doing here now, when he should be at work in Vienna? Colour rushed to her face.

'Are you all right?' Noah asked urgently, not missing her sudden flare of colour.

'Yes,' she said. 'Yes,' she repeated, and, because he looked so concerned, 'You're not the only one allowed emotions.' She smiled.

'You feel—hmm—a tiny bit ''emotional'' about me?' he asked, his eyes steady on hers.

She wasn't quite sure how to answer him. No way did she want to give away too much. But, then again, Noah had said he was being totally honest and, whatever happened, didn't she owe him total honesty in return? 'A—bit,' she admitted, finding she couldn't be as hugely honest as she should have been in this delicate area—though aware now that she was going to tell him about the baby before he left. But, as another thought suddenly struck her, 'You're not just saying all this—um, liking me and everything—just to make me feel better?' she questioned abruptly, not wanting to believe that he was, but finding it incredible enough that he was here with her now, and starting to feel uncertain.

Noah stared at her, his expression serious. Then, softly,

he asked, 'Does it make you feel better to know that I like you—very, very much?'

Oh, Noah, don't do this to me. 'It's—er—always nicer to be liked than disliked,' she prevaricated, and Noah looked at her for long, long unspeaking seconds. Then Elexa had very good reason to be glad she was sitting propped up in his arm in her bed because, had she been standing when next he spoke, she felt sure she would have dropped in shock.

Because, after long moments of just looking into her wide brown eyes, Noah seemed to take a long pull of breath, and what he said was, 'And how would you feel, my dearest Elexa, if I told you that I more than like you very, very much?' His dearest Elexa? Her mouth went dry, and that was before he quietly added, 'And that the fact of the matter is...' he paused '...I—love you, very, very much.'

Feeling as if her heart would leap straight out of her body, Elexa stared at him dumbstruck. 'You—love me?' she gasped.

'With everything that's in me,' Noah confirmed.

He loved her! He *loved* her! Noah loved her—very, very much! She couldn't believe it. He *was* just saying that to make her feel better, she was sure of it now. 'Steady on, Noah,' she managed to find her voice, it taking her all her time to stay steady herself. 'You'll be asking me to marry you next!'

'I'm sure as hell not going to tolerate a divorce!' he replied shortly, before she could blink

'You're not? I thought you were!' she answered, startled. 'I thought...'

'What did you think?' Noah prompted when she seemed stuck for words.

'Well—I...' Had he really said he loved her and didn't want a divorce? She started to tremble in his arms.

'Oh, my dear. What is it?' he asked, feeling her tremble and perhaps thinking it was part of her being unwell.

'It's...' The words would not come. Not to tell him that she was having his child anyway. But, 'Well, if we're talking complete honesty here...'

'We are,' Noah said firmly.

'Th-then, I'll admit, when you didn't—um—contact me—you know—two weeks ago—W-Wednesday...'

'When it was your fertile time?' He didn't back away from letting her know he knew what she was referring to.

'You deliberately didn't contact me. It *was* deliberate, wasn't it?'

'It was,' he answered, and confused her totally. Confirming he had known what the dates were, but had deliberately kept away, he then gently kissed her lips!

'I thought then that you'd gone off the idea, and were about to tell me you wanted a divorce,' she brought out, feeling utterly lost.

'You mean—you'd no idea how I felt about you?' He looked as surprised as she felt startled.

'As in—you l-love me?' she whispered.

'Love and adore you,' Noah breathed. 'Oh, my love, there's such a wealth of feeling in me for you, I haven't known whether I'm on my head or heels.'

She stared at him, joy pushing to get through—common sense holding it firmly down. 'You do?' she questioned. 'Then why...?'

'Why have I kept away from you?' Tenderly he kissed her again, then he smiled a shade self-deprecatingly. 'At first it took me by surprise. I didn't want any emotional entanglements, didn't have time or space for such nonsense.'

'That's wh-what I overheard you say.'

'And meant,' he admitted. 'So why do I feel so proud to have you, my bride, on my arm? Why am I lunching at the Montgomery as often as I'm able—instead of once every blue moon?'

That struck a chord. 'It—um—couldn't have been because you were hoping to see me there—accidentally?' Elexa suggested shyly.

'Certainly not,' he lied, and kissed her gently again in case she believed that lie. 'So, if I don't feel any special urge to see you whenever I can, why am I calling here to tell you of Sarah's engagement dinner at my parents' home when I could more easily have picked up a telephone?'

'You liked me, you said,' Elexa murmured, joy inside straining at the leash.

'And that night, that night of the dinner for Sarah and Lewis, I discovered—I loved you,' Noah confessed.

'You—how? When?' Without her knowing it she had placed an arm around his waist—she needed it there; she needed something to hold on to.

'If you remember, and I'm sure you do,' he smiled, 'we were not going to stay in Sussex overnight. But while I could have taken Scott Wheeler concentrating his attentions solely on you—I couldn't take you smiling and laughing with him all evening.'

Her mouth fell open a fraction. 'You were—jealous?' she gasped, her eyes huge in her face.

'Not admitting it—then,' Noah replied. 'But—' he grinned '—peeved enough to think Tough when I knew you didn't want to stay the night.'

Elexa was too thrilled to know that Noah thought enough of her to be jealous to be upset at his Tough remark. But, remembering how wonderful it had been to be in his arms, 'You didn't stay mad at me,' she murmured.

'How could I? You smiled your beautiful smile, and laughed your lovely laugh when you told me you'd refer Wheeler to me when he phoned, and I—I fell heart and soul in love with you.'

'Oh, Noah,' she sighed.

'Do you mind?' he asked tenderly.

'Not a scrap,' she replied breathlessly, and, as if she was a piece of fragile porcelain, was tenderly kissed.

'Dare I ask if you have any feeling for me—apart from liking me "a bit"?' Noah asked.

'Yes, of course,' she answered shyly, but because of that shyness hurried on, 'I truly thought you wanted a divorce—now.'

'What in thunder gave you that idea?'

'You—er—we hadn't been in contact,' she reminded him, and he groaned.

'Forgive me, sweetheart. All this is so new to me. Half my time I've been in panic, in fear you'd want nothing to do with me should I dare to tell you anything of my feelings. While the rest of the time I've been crashing through my workload, completing my commitments without making fresh ones, so that I would shortly be able to stay in London near to you.'

'You wanted to be near to me?' Elexa questioned. Then, shaking her head, had to query, 'But you were in London. You said so only last Saturday.'

'And it was agony not contacting you,' he supplied. 'But I dared not.'

She was flummoxed. 'I don't understand,' she had to admit.

'My darling, I love you, but I didn't know how you felt about me. So, since to my mind I'd done things totally the wrong way round, marrying first when I should have wooed you beforehand, I decided to put matters right by clearing up my workload so that I'd be free to—hopefully, and if you would allow it—come courting.'

'Oh, Noah,' she whispered.

'Sweet love,' he said tenderly. 'Then the devil of it was that, when I did have a window in my workload, it coincided with a time when I knew you might conceive my child. It was important to me that you should know it was you I wanted, and not just because of the reason I married you.'

'A baby, a child,' Elexa said faintly.

'Forgive me, darling?' Noah requested. 'But I think you're aware that there's a very special kind of physical chemistry between us. We weren't supposed to make love that Saturday down at my parents; it just—happened. I've wanted to tell you how I felt about you, but didn't want to rush it. So what if you became pregnant before I felt able to tell you of my love for you? You're sensitive, my love. I wanted you to know that it was you I wanted, not the son I married you for. Besides which,' he said with a tender smile, 'I want you to myself for as long as I can.'

'That's—w-wonderful,' she choked, her voice all wobbly, knowing as she did that she had better tell him—and soon!

'I'm glad you think so. This is such an intense emotion—it had me scared.'

'Scared! You?'

'I can't begin to tell you. There was I, desperate to see you, yet scared of being alone with you in case I got carried away with the pure delight of having you near. To have dinner with your parents seemed a safe enough idea—but then I found I didn't want to part from you.'

'You didn't?' She stared at him, recalling how on their return he had kissed her goodnight outside this apartment block and then, without saying another word, had gone quickly back to his car.

Noah shook his head. 'I wanted to come in with you—to hold you through the night. It seemed to me then as I drove home that the sooner I got my workload dealt with the better. My dear,' he went on, 'barring today, when the moment I knew you were ill I delegated my second-in-command to give my speech, I have honoured all my work commitments. So—' he broke off to gently kiss her forehead '—do I have your permission to come courting?'

'Y-you don't want a divorce?'

'You've not been listening,' he rebuked her sternly. 'Mrs Peverelle, I should like to be married to you for ever.' Oh, Noah. 'I asked you a little while ago if you had any feeling for me apart from liking me "a bit". You said "Yes, of course!" You wouldn't care to add anything to that, I suppose?'

'Oh, Noah!' The words would not stay down. Incredibly, it seemed to her that he was actually a touch anxious as he waited for her answer. 'I've loved you from that first night when, instead of throwing me out because I "couldn't", you offered to make me some tea—and actually laughed.'

He looked stunned. 'Since then?' he asked incredulously. 'You've loved me—since then?'

'Since then.' She smiled. 'You're not the only one who's found a reason to lunch or be walking past the Montgomery on the off-chance...' And suddenly she was held fast against his heart, locked to him for long soothing minutes.

'Oh, sweetheart,' he breathed when at length he drew back. Tenderly he kissed her, and then gravely stated, 'You're starting to look more like my Elexa, but, not to put too fine a point on it, I don't think I'm going to be able to hide for much longer that I am going quietly out of my head worrying about you. Could you not give me a clue what's wrong with you so I can get the best specialist to come and treat you?'

'I…' She tried to get started, tried to tell him, but a mixture of shyness and uncertainty held her back.

'My love, believe me, this is no time for modesty.' Noah tried to help her out. 'Can you not tell me of these "women's problems" that you've never had to be off work with before?' he urged.

'I—um—I've n-never been married before either,' she managed, and found Noah was as sharp and as quick on the uptake as ever.

'This, you being ill, has something to do with our being married?' he discerned, and looked so seriously worried and horrified as he questioned, 'I'm the cause?' that she hurriedly rushed to explain.

'I'm half the cause,' she said quickly. 'And there's nothing wrong that isn't absolutely quite normal.'

'Go on,' he pressed, the strain he was under starting to show.

Elexa quickly obeyed. 'It appears I'm not as numerate as we both thought I was.'

'You're—not?'

'I made a mistake in my calculations,' she confessed. 'Well, it *is* new territory for me,' she defended. And when Noah stared at her, his serious grey eyes fixed on hers, she went on, 'And, because of that, I now have to drink orange juice instead of the occasional gin and tonic, which I would much prefer.'

Noah's brow went up, and she wasn't sure he hadn't lost some of his colour. But his voice was tightly controlled when quietly, his grip on her tensing, he questioned, 'What are you telling me, Elexa?'

'That I feel sick the moment my feet touch the floor. That the person who first named it m-morning sickness must have been totally unaware that it seems to last most of the day. That—'

'Morning sickness!' Noah exclaimed, looking absolutely thunderstruck. 'You're—you're—having my baby?' he questioned hoarsely.

Elexa nodded. 'Do you mind?'

'Mind? Oh, my love! Oh, let me hold you.' And with that he held her tightly up against his heart once more. 'You're having my baby,' he breathed exultantly, as if he could barely believe it. 'Our baby,' he said in wonder, and for long, long minutes he just held her, sometimes planting a kiss in her hair sometimes kissing the side of her face. 'And this is what's wrong with you?' he demanded to know, pulling back. 'Having my baby has thrown your system out of gear?'

'You could say that.' She smiled. 'I managed to get into work yesterday. This morning—it was just impossible.'

'Oh, sweet love,' he crooned, 'and I did this to you.'

'I don't remember complaining,' she laughed, her heart so full of love for him.

'It happened down in Sussex, didn't it?' he stated. 'When I loved you and you loved me.'

'Oh Noah,' she cried in delight. 'Our baby was conceived with love for each other in our hearts!'

For long moments then they just sat and held each other, then Noah was drawing back to examine her face. 'How are you feeling now?' he asked.

'Given that I'm a bit wary of trying to put my feet on the floor—on top of the world.' She grinned, and was held safe by him for more minutes.

'How long have you known?' he asked, and, as alert as ever, 'You chose orange juice last Saturday!' he recalled.

Elexa smiled, and as her confidence grew she was happy to tell him, 'I hadn't a clue until the other Sunday, when I was idly checking everything and I suddenly realised...I did a test the next day and my doctor confirmed it last Friday.'

'Oh, darling, and you've kept it to yourself—' He broke off. 'You *did* intend to tell me?' he questioned, a shade severely.

'I did think about telling you last Saturday, only...' His groan halted her.

'Only I told you last Saturday that to have a son wasn't the best idea I'd ever had.'

'You didn't know,' she quickly excused him. 'And I'd started to have maternal feelings of a strength I'd never expected. And, while I knew you'd every right to know, just as I knew that at some time I would tell you, I've also discovered that no matter what we agreed about—er—your son—living permanently with you—I just won't be able to part from him. I'm sorry, but, knowing the way I feel now, I just don't know whatever made me think that I could.'

'You won't have to, sweet love,' Noah soothed. 'It's *our* baby.'

'You don't mind about it? Er—you're all right about the baby?' she asked tentatively, and Noah bent to gently kiss her.

'I couldn't be more pleased,' he assured her softly. 'Or more proud. But my first concern at the moment, sweetheart, is you.'

'I'll be fine,' she promised him. 'This awful sickness doesn't last long they say.'

'Let's hope *they* are right. In the meantime, my darling, I'm going to take good care of you. Now, are you coming home with me? If you don't want to risk testing your feet to the floor I'll carry you to my car, no problem. Or would you prefer me to move in here with you while we look for that place in the country?'

'Oh, Noah,' Elexa cried, suddenly feeling she could not only put her feet to the floor, but that she could dance a jig as well. 'You w-want us to live together?'

'I'll settle for nothing less,' he replied firmly. 'You're my wife.' And he owned, 'While I confess I thought I'd considered every angle before we married, it never even remotely came to me that I might fall in love with the woman I married, but that is what happened. I love and want you with me with all that I have, my dearest Elexa,' he said, tenderly brushing her hair back from her face. 'I want you with me, to have and to hold, to love and to cherish, and to guard and keep you safe with me.' Elexa felt near to tears again. It was almost as if Noah had just renewed his marriage vows. 'Would you now be so heart-less as to tell me I must live alone?' he asked.

Elexa looked at him with nothing but love in her eyes. 'I wouldn't dream of saying any such thing,' she answered lovingly. 'Um—may I come home with you?'

Noah gazed at her for long adoring moments. 'Sweet darling,' he breathed, 'you're wonderful,' and, gently, he kissed her.

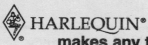

HARLEQUIN®
makes any time special—online...

shop eHarlequin

- ♥ Find all the new Harlequin releases at everyday great discounts.
- ♥ Try before you buy! Read an excerpt from the latest Harlequin novels.
- ♥ Write an online review and share your thoughts with others.

reading room

- ♥ Read our Internet exclusive daily and weekly online serials, or vote in our interactive novel.
- ♥ Talk to other readers about your favorite novels in our Reading Groups.

- ♥ Take our Choose-a-Book quiz to find the series that matches you!

authors' alcove

- ♥ Find out interesting tidbits and details about your favorite authors' lives, interests and writing habits.
- ♥ Ever dreamed of being an author? Enter our Writing Round Robin. The Winning Chapter will be published online! Or review our writing guidelines for submitting your novel.

All this and more available at
www.eHarlequin.com
on Women.com Networks

HINTB1R

Harlequin Romance®
Love affairs that
last a lifetime.

HARLEQUIN *Presents*~
Seduction and passion
guaranteed.

◈ *Harlequin*®
® *Historical*
Historical
Romantic
Adventure.

HARLEQUIN®
Temptation.
Sassy, sexy, seductive!

HARLEQUIN *Super*ROMANCE®
Emotional,
exciting,
unexpected.

HARLEQUIN®
AMERICAN *Romance*®
Heart, home
& happiness.

HARLEQUIN®
Duets™
Romantic comedy.

HARLEQUIN®
INTRIGUE®
Breathtaking
romantic suspense.

HARLEQUIN® *Blaze*™
Red-Hot Reads.

◈ HARLEQUIN®
Makes any time special ®

Visit us at www.eHarlequin.com

Together for the first time in one Collector's Edition!

New York Times bestselling authors

Barbara Delinsky

Catherine Coulter

Linda Howard

Forever Yours

A special trade-size volume containing three complete novels that showcase the passion, imagination and stunning power that these talented authors are famous for.

Coming to your favorite retail outlet in December 2001.

HARLEQUIN®
Makes any time special ®

Visit us at www.eHarlequin.com

PHFY